Kat

I hate people.

I don't know if I'm just cynical or my anger is due to the fact that I'm stuck in this crowded airport that smells like that obscure church your grandma takes you to once a year.

My mom thought it would be an absolute great idea to send me, the sad kid in the family who suffers from a mix of horrible social skills AND an anxiety disorder, to the airport and pick up my older cousins from London who I haven't seen in five years. They're here for their friends' wedding which we weren't invited to, but they decided to visit us and stay at our house (for an entire month) while they're in the city. Okay, I guess, but as you can imagine, I am in a pretty tense situation right now.

As I'm about to projectile vomit all over this Starbucks booth, my phone lights up with Isaac's contact. Thank God.

"Hey, I'll be right there." I say into my ear as I make my way to their gate. How the hell am I gonna get through this? I haven't seen these guys since my emo phase. My hair is obviously ridden of the bright red streaks I paid my aunt to put in. I don't straighten my hair that often anymore; I just let it fall in its natural, frizzy waves. My second cousin,

Sarah, has always loved my hair. The redheaded sweetheart would bring back pure coconut oil spray back from her yearly vacations to California, where her girlfriend, Antigany (*we call her "Tig" for short*) is from. Tig transferred to Brooklyn in middle school and moved in with a foster family, so she accompanies her when she goes home to visit. She has some life.

Where as I, despite having a best friend who hangs out with me occasionally between sucking face with her moody boyfriend, am left to feel like I have absolutely no one.

Sorry. Oversharing.

"KATHERINE!" A loud British voice boomed, snapping me out of my deep reverie. I turned to see my two big cousins, looking even more grown up than last with their dark hair fluffed to the side and tight designer clothing clinging to their bodies I can tell that their male modeling career has finally paid off.

Anthony, the slightly taller blue eyed one tackled me over the plastic stools first, embracing me in his tight hug that smelled of tea and cologne. Isaac with his brown eyes and sharp attitude followed after, almost knocking me down to the cheap plastic seats.

"I've seen you finally gotten rid of that horrid

hairstyle." Isaac remarked, slinging his duffle bag over his shoulder. I stood on my toes and ruffled my hand over his punk-band-like fringe so he would shut up.

"Hold on guys, I need to get an uber." I say, reaching in the pocket of my denim jacket pulling out my phone, dialing the number.
"Holy fuck, you don't drive yet?" Anthony asks, rearranging his luggage. Great. How am I supposed to explain that I, a 17 year old kid am too fucking scared of getting behind a wheel? One of my worst panic attacks was when I had my driver's test. I think I scared the poor teacher to death when I jumped out of the moving Honda civic and ran three blocks home. I still don't know what happened to him.

"Yeah, just…hung-over!" I mentally smacked myself. Hung-over? Really, Kat? Of all excuses in the world, the first one to come to the front of your mind was 'I'm hung-over? Like they're gonna even believe, you, of all kids, were out and drinking. Let's see how you get yourself out of this one.

"Nice." He just chuckles, letting it go and ruffling my hair as the black sedan starts to roll up in front of us.

"Anthony and I are going to that frat party at house 86" Isaac said, reminding me of the empty house two blocks from here with a yellow 86 spray painted on the door. Rumor has it that it's supposedly haunted by a prostitute. When he came to live with me during the summer of fourth grade, we would always hide in the bushes in front of the sinister residence with 'ghost hunting equipment' strapped to our belts and would wait until we saw anything suspicious. We never saw a shadow, or even heard footsteps, but we still had an amusing time just sitting there late at night. "Wanna come?

"Me? Partying?" I remarked, my eyes not drifting away from the editing screen on my laptop. "Funny."

"Katheriiiiiiiiiiine." He dragged out my full name. "You need to get out."

"I get out just fine on my own, thank you very much." I respond as I drag the last clip from my walk downtown up to the effects bar, adding a bit of brightness to enhance the sunlight. Truth is, i don't get out. Not even for something as normal as school, because I've been doing online school since i was 15.

He snorted. "Dude, I love you, but anyone who is inside on a Friday night editing a montage of ethereal nature shots to LL Cool J songs most likely needs an outing." He says, handing me my leather jacket before putting on his own. "This is a cry for help."

I knew I didn't have a say in this because Isaac is the most stubborn person I have ever met. Once, when we were little, I told him he couldn't eat play doh because the TV spot specifically said "Fun to play with, not to eat!" He then looked me dead in the eye, rolled up the purple clay into a ball, and took a huge bite. After he finished the entire portion, he leaned over to me, and whispered "The system knows nothing."

"Fine, you fuck." I stood up, shrugging on the leather jacket and flipping my unkempt hair out of the collar. "Only if you pitch that hot director my screenplay for the untitled anti-hero thing." "Katherine, you're 17." He says, heading towards my door. "I'm not gonna shove a screenplay in my bosses' husbands' face that was written by someone who isn't even legal yet."

"Fock off, mate."

"I don't fucking talk like that." He sighed, opening the door. "That's Cockney. By the way, it's a halfoween party. So, probably gonna get weird."

I groaned and shut the door. Halfoween is an annual tradition in the frat community here in the boroughs. It's held on June 1st, which is the halfway point in the countdown to Halloween. The tradition is that you have to dress half of your body in a elaborate costume, and the other half in your regular clothes. The last time I went, I was 14 and dragged by my friend Ariel to her brothers' because I owed her a favor. Long story short, I didn't even have a license and I didn't have much accuracy, but I ended up being the designated driver for way too many people that night. Ariel's' brother covered me when I got questioned (because why the fuck is a 5'3 scrawny kid behind the wheel of a grand prius at 12 in the morning) and told them I was their chauffeur who came from a tiny island in Europe where people grow shorter than the average human, called 'The British Tin-iles." For some reason, the amateur cop was convinced and I drove five people home that night.

That night was the only time in my life when I truly felt alive, as fucking cliché as it sounds. I sprung free of any controls I had on the universe, and just let myself free of overthinking too much.

I wish I could turn off my mind like that still.

In fact, I wish my whole life was like that night.

But no, this is reality. Shitty, toxic, fucking reality. That would be some sort of chummy gummy bear fantasy world, really. Tragically, I only exist in the pages of a realistic fiction story. You can thank this dumbass author for that one, kids. You wanted a relatable book.

Alex

Okay, ouch.

Did I just get slapped?

I take in my surroundings as the initial shock fades away and I remember where I am. I'm at the small boutique my girlfriend, Felicia, works at downtown. I get up, rubbing my cheek gently as I remind myself why I'm here.

To support my girlfriend's promotion from a random cashier to the manager- wait, who the fuck slapped me in the face?

I look up to see Felicia's best friend, *cough*, minion, Meagan, hovering over me. She's so close to my face I can see where she forgot to blend her bronzer.

"I can't believe you said that!"

And I can't believe you're allowed to buy cosmetics with the way you make yourself look like the deformed daughter of Donald Trump, but, you do you.

"I said what?"

"That if Felicia ever pulls said bullshit again, you'll leave!" She says, her stubby hands waving dramatically.

Oh, that's right. Felicia was openly talking about our argument last week to her minions-in front of me, may I add. Shouldn't that shit be kept private?

We've been arguing so much over stupid shit lately, I can hardly keep track of what she's talking about. We've been together for a year, but lately it seems like the shit she used to love about me she got tired of.

I swore to myself I would never change for anyone, though. Even before I got a girlfriend. How is that fair to yourself if you have a perfectly useful mind and it's not being liberated?
Fuck, sorry, I sound like a Shakespeare douche. I get caught up in my own dialogue sometimes.

Holy shit, I do sound like a douche.

Anyway, back to my Armageddon.

Felicia is sitting on the pink sofa crying, and I feel a

little guilty. I do love her, I mean, at least I think I still do.

I ran out the door and over to Rachel's coffee shop. Rachel is probably the only sane person on my block, and she's kind of like the older sibling I never had. Ever since me and my family moved here from Nevada, she's pretty much been the only person I could really talk to, although I can't see her often since she's always working.

"You gotta break up with her." She sighs, shaking a bottle of whipped cream to put on my hot chocolate. "And why the hell are ya drinkin' hot chocolate in June."

"It comforts me." I take the styrofoam cup from her and give her 5 bucks, thanking her.

I love the feeling of hot chocolate in June.

Later that day, I pulled up to the all-too-familiar house 86 with my ridiculous long blue coat tripping me over my own two feet.

Fuck last minute costume ideas.

I open the door for Felicia, and silently thank God that the familiar fluffy purple head that belonged to Matt is leaning against the outdoor frame, each limb stacked in Calvin Klein panties and smoking a cigarette.

"Who. The fuck. Are you." He hisses through a drag.

"Dude, seriously?" I asked, twirling around like a bride who just chosen her dress in front of him so he could see my sick coat tail. "What's my name?"

"Alexander." He ruffles his cosmic-like fluffy hair.

"Yeah." I nodded towards him. "I'm Hamilton! First secretary of treasury of our gr-"

"Jesus Christ, why do I hang out with you."

"Says the guy with bright ass hair with underwear all over his body." I snorted. "Look, it was last minute, but, he was, like, the coolest New Yorker to ever exist. Plus, I feel noble as fuck in this tarp."

"You know there are cooler famous New Yorkers who live within blocks from you who weren't shot in the fucking ribs by his buddy?" He raised an eyebrow. "And, I'm a panty magnet. Found a few of these in the back seat of my car." He winks and I chuckle, shaking my head. I've known Matt for two years, being the only kid willing to look past his purple hair bad boy façade thing. I don't think he's ever had a constant fuck buddy or a place to do it other than the back of his Benz. Christ, he needs to clean out his car. "Anyway, how was your day?"

"Well, Felicia-"

"LALALALALALA," He plugged his ears and I rolled my eyes. "I call Switzerland."

Of course he does. Felicia is his friend too, i met him through her.

"Come on, man, I need to let this shit out or I might explode."

"That's what she said." He snorted, patting me on the back.

"That wasn't even close to a sexual innuendo." I groaned. If you took a shot every time I rolled my eyes at this dickweed, you would be on the floor.

He paused for a second. "You're a fucking sexual innuendo." He stood on his toes and flicked my forehead, just to check out someone behind me. He murmured something about how Daddy's home and I almost gagged.

I lost Matt, Can't talk to Felicia, who is literally grinding into another guy like a fucking screwdriver. I'm not even gonna bother at this point. I can't ignore the pang of jealousy and annoyance that washes over me, but at the same time, I need to be free from her acrylic-nail talons for a little bit. I keep telling myself I love her, and I do but- fuck, I'm over sharing. Just met you. Sorry.

I squeeze my way through the crowd of intoxicated dancers, bumping into a few girls dressed in skimpy cat costumes occasionally. I'm not one to criticize what people wear, but like, you can't get any more creative?

Granted, most kids only come to these parties to get laid, so, I guess they're doing a good job. I've only slept with Felicia in my life, and-fuck, over sharing again. Gotta stop that.
I look out at the front yard, searching for a spot where I could sit and be left alone. Two guys dressed as glam rockers are making out against the garage, a group of anime kids are playing spin the bottle on the driveway and I slowly walk away, knowing I don't want any part of this. You don't fuck with the anime kids. Who even invited them?

I made an unintelligible noise out of frustration and rubbed my temples, taking a seat next to a girl in a leather jacket on the steps leading to the house, the area being empty. She drummed on the tile with a rolled up piece of red construction paper as she kept her eyes on the horizon. "Can I help you?" God, I hope so.

Kat

Have I told anyone how much I hate parties?

I came outside to get some air after too many intoxicated people crowded around me. I've grown to not be okay around drunk people. Maybe it's because I wish I had the courage to actually get drunk, but now their slurred words and lack of control over their own minds make me feel claustrophobic.

God, I'm a prude, aren't I?

Shut up, subconscious, that's misogynistic bullshit and you know it. I've learned in my lovely years of high school that guys will only see you as two things-a prude or a slut. If you've had sex and partied, you're a slut. If you're a virgin and stay in at night, you're a prude. You can't win.

I take my cup of ginger ale and tell Anthony that I'm going outside, and he nods at me as he continues to make out with a girl dressed as an angel.

I need someone to invent tear-free Lysol safe for eyes.

I sit on the tile steps in front of the door, trying to slow my breathing down by looking at the stars.

Then, an idiot decides to come and sit next to me. Greeeaaaattt.

"Can I help you?" I asked him, trying to cover the fact that my breathing is unsteady. I tried not to look interested, but the guy was wearing a fucking colonial coat and I had to bite the corner of my lip to keep from smiling.

"No one can at this point." He mumbles, and I sigh, readying myself for a random stranger to tell me about their life problems. Forgive me, but I don't give a shit. He jerked his chin towards me."What are you supposed to be?"

I picked up my "lightsaber" and showed him. "I'm a really low budget darth vader."

Then he started laughing. Like, really laughing .His smile went really wide, and his elfish nose scrunched up while his blue eyes crinkled. "That's great," He says, calming down his childish giggles. "I needed that."

I frowned. "Okay, who are you supposed to be, Thomas Jefferson?"

"God no," He winced, buttoning himself up. "I'm Alexander Hamilton."

I snickered a bit at his history appreciation.

A wave of silence washed over us and you could practically taste the awkwardness in the air.

I was just about to text Anthony when a purple head of hair caught my eye.

"I'm Alex by the way." He mumbled, opening his wine cooler with his pinky ring.

I've never seen anyone other than my great aunt Delphine wear a pinky ring before. I guess pinky fingers are a pretty overlooked place to put a ring.

"Katherine."

I look back ahead of us and see a dude that's gotta be at most 14 walking towards me, drinking champagne by the bottle. Fucking disgusting, yet, respect.

"Hey babe," He said, winking at me. Greeeaaaattt. Time to talk to someone again. "What's a pretty thing like-"

"Say one more word and I won't hesitate to make you cry so hard the laws of anatomy will reverse and tears will be dripping out of your asshole." I deadpanned, keeping my eyes narrowed on the house across the street, not wanting to look at the toddler.

Jesus Christ. Where the fuck did that come from?

It was like my anxious, annoyed state conjured up graphic insults and became more intimidating than my right mind ever could. I groan and turn my head, just to see Hamilton laughing again. He tucked his lanky legs under his arms and his head was buried between his knees, coming up to breathe occasionally. "You," He hiccupped, scrunching up his nose again. "The earth doesn't deserve you. You're too great for us mediocre humans, Kat." I raised an eyebrow at his words and the nickname he gave me, processing whatever the hell was trying to say. No one has ever thought to call me such a simple name like Kat before, but something in me liked the way Alex said it. It's stupid, but, it made me feel less boring than I actually am.

"KATHERINE RUDNITSKY!" I heard Isaac shout from across the lawn, taking his fedora off. Thank god. "The cops are coming, stick with me!"

Fuck, cops make me nervous. I ran towards Isaac, texting Anthony and a cab pulled up in front of us. Anthony was already in the front seat waiting for us, rambling about how he couldn't find us and how terrified he was. My heart was practically beating out of my chest and I felt like this goddamn taxi was closing in on me. Isaac takes notice of my snapping fingers, a habit I formed when I was first diagnosed with an anxiety disorder, and hands me a piece of gum from his pocket.

"You're okay, Katherine." He says, in attempt to comfort me. "We're almost home."

The next few minutes were a blur of me trying not to pass out and Isaac trying to comfort me until I got outside in the fresh June air. I took a deep breath and walked over to my front door, opening it for Isaac and Anthony and to my luck, my mom was waiting for me at the dining room table, clutching our dog in her arms.

"Did you have fun, sweetie?" She asks, putting Zeus down on the floor so he could greet me properly by rubbing his fluffy paws all over my ripped jeans. "Wasn't it nice to go out?"

"Yeah, mom, it was great." I lied, jogging upstairs to avoid conversation. I love her, and she means well, but I just came down from a panic attack and I don't want to talk to anyone.

I jumped down on my bed and felt something jingle in my pocket. I furrow my eyebrows and fix my eyes on my light blue wall as I fish around in my jacket pocket. I feel something small and smooth and I pull it out, my eyes immediately recognizing what it is.

The pinky ring.

Alex

The bold, curly haired girl called Kat turned around at the sound of her name being called followed by sirens.

And the cops are here, just as expected.

As much as I don't want to get arrested, I want to keep talking to her. People like her want me to bring out my inner cheesy poet. I don't know much about her, but I do know I have never seen her smile and I want to be worthy of an amused grin from her.

Okay, think. Wait! What are you doing, you assface, you have a girl- No. Don't think.

I choose to act on emotional impulse and take the ring off my finger and slip it into her pocket as she gets up from the stoop we're sitting on, something at the back of my mind already telling me that I'm going to regret this. That's the ring that belonged to my father before he died, and I just gave it to some random girl I just met at a party. What the hell is wrong with me?

I quickly dialed Felicia's number, and in any other

situation I would have laughed at the irony but her phone went straight to voicemail. I shook my head in desperation and narrowed my eyes until I spotted Matt in the crowd, utterly wasted and tripping over his own two feet as the Drake song that was playing cut short, following a shout of "THE EAGLE HAS LANDED!"
And that's when the hell really let loose.

Floods of sweaty, panicked bodies seemed to pour out of the living room at once; clouding over my vision and making me lose sight of Matt, who was probably already gone.
Shit.

And this, this is where I hear it.

"Are you stupid or something?" Felicia's shrilly voice cuts through my ear drums like a dozen knives- as if I wasn't stressed enough. I have not been dropped from her talons after all. As I'm racing towards the back kitchen door to plan to jump to my Matt's house next door through the backyard, her ass is trailing me with more lectures of how stupid I must be that I "flat-left" her when I showed up. Meanwhile, it was her who didn't want anything to do with me tonight as I'm perching my boot-clad feet on the brown fence, heart set on getting to the other side. As I take the leap from the top of the fence, she's mumbling something about how I'm completely worthless just like this relationship. I land on my feet, surprisingly, and sigh deeply while closing my eyes.

That hurt like a bitch.

It would only hurt like a mega-bitch if I wasn't used to it already.

Why do I put up with this, you ask? Why don't I just break up with her?

Well, I don't know the exact answer either. I just keep hoping that this is a phase she's going through and things will go back to the things they were at the beginning of our relationship, where she made me feel happy and valid and important.

I just hang on to her because I need familiarity. I need to still feel important, and I used to get that with her. But I can't confront her about it, because she gets crazy, but I can't leave her, because I still love her. She's really all I've got left that (was) is okay in my life. She was the first person to really notice me when I moved here. I need her, I need her to feel important, which sounds pathetic, but I just keep hoping things will go back to the way they were.
Shitty thing about hope, though. It's false, most of the time. And false hope is the most toxic drug you could ever inject into your bloodstream.

I don't even bother to alert Matt that I am laying on his hammock in his backyard as my teary eyes got bored of looking at the stars painted in the sky and closed down for the night.

Kat

I woke up the next morning with a nagging feeling at the back of my mind.

I got up out of bed as soon as my eyes opened, feeling urgently like I needed to do something. I looked around my room frantically as the events of last night flooded to the front of my mind. My leather jacket was lying on the floor and I practically darted like a madman to pick it up and look through the pockets.

The ring was still there.

I don't get why I was so excited, but maybe it had to deal with the fact that returning the ring will force me into getting out of the house. Often times on weekends I feel so alone and I unwillingly turn into an existential nihilist. When there is nothing to do and my mind is run down, those are the times I feel so trapped in my own mind. It makes me feel so claustrophobic in my own damn world.

I'm pretty sure I saw Alex talking to Matt last night,

who is Ariel's on and off boyfriend, and his house is just down the block from house 86. He's agitating though, so if I'm gonna go to his door to drop this off it better be worth it.

I pick up my phone and dial Ariel's number without a second thought and told her I needed a ride to dbag's house, no questions asked. She agreed, as long as "we stop by that little book shop on the way back. I need to get a book of those dumb modern hipster trash poems for my dumb hipster trash class."

If you think I'm elitist, you should see the people I surround myself with.
Anyway, next thing I know, I'm at shiny happy purple's door.

"Oh, god-"He says groggily, rubbing his eyes.

"What could you possibly want from me, besides a knife in my throat?"

"Funny," I said in that sarcastic monotone voice that leaves my lips so frequently now. I fish the ring out of the back pocket of my shorts and shove it in front of him. "I believe this belongs to your friend, Alex. He slipped it into my pocket and, assuming as we just met last night, I thought he would like it back, and I don't know where he even came from, so I'm giving it to you to give to him."

He took the ring out of my hands and examined it, cocking his eyebrow up at me. "Yeah, you just missed him, actually. Fell asleep on my hammock, woke up covered in pollen. Classic."

He chuckled to himself, handing the ring back to me. "I'm not going to give it to him though."
I gave him a look like what, dude, why?

"Alex seemed genuinely happy last night when he was talking to you. I'm pretty sure you are the ideal girl I designed for Alex. Good job." He flashed me smile and chugged the rest of his beer. (Yes, at 11 in the morning.)

So guys design dream significant others for their best friends, too.

"Plus, Ariel tells me you're depressed. And you seemed like you needed that talk with a random person. You're glowing today!" He went to pinch my cheeks and I smacked his hand away. "Point is, you made each other feel good, and fate will bring you two together because I am almost sure you are soul mates, although he has a girlfriend-" Wait, why did my heart sink in disappointment when he said that? "Eh, he's not hitting that right anyway."

"Thank you, Mr. Secrets of the Universe; I'll leave this to fate!" I gave him a fake smile and thumbs up, walking down his driveway. Guess this guy isn't getting his ring back any time soon. Whatever "fate" is, it's never been on my side. Not to say that everything sucks, either, it's just not how my life goes. My life is the same every day. No big things. No surprises. It's like my life's one big long grey day with only short breaks of sun peaking through the clouds over my brain.

"I don't appreciate the sarcasm!" He yells as I get back in Ariel's car. "Although I'm sure Alex wouldn't mind!"

"Why is he yelling like that?" Ariel asks and rolls her eyes, mumbling about how she can't believe she ever even slept with him.

"Let's just go." I say, buckling my seat belt, just wanting to get out of there. She puts the Pulp Fiction soundtrack back in the built-in CD player and sped away.

We arrived at the Littletown Book House ten minutes later with McDonalds fries in our hands, not caring about the fact that it's 11 in the morning.

Ariel made her way to the poetry section all the way by the corner of the cozy wooden walls, leaving me in the center of the store to do what I want. I chose to sit in the bright purple bean bag in the corner, where I hide my favorite, most pretentious books under. I pull a dusty paperback copy of The Outsiders out from the comfy spot, finishing my fries as I read about high school kids at social war.

The tale is cliché and age old, but this book taught me a lot. Especially the author, S.E. Hinton, wrote and published that book at 16.

It makes me think I could really do this. Write a movie at 17. It's like every time I read The Outsiders I think of my dreams and goals and I become very motivated.

Anyway, I'm deep into the beginning when I feel a delicate tap on my shoulder.
Now, guys, before I turn around and face the one thing that changed my life forever, I want you to know that I was not ready for this.

Anyway, I whip my head around, there he is.

"KAT!" He says rather loudly, flashing that boyish grin again.

"Oh, uhhh, hey!" The words struggle to stumble out of my mouth as I'm faced with the presence of the one person that seemed interesting in this whole goddam part of town.

Jesus Christ, Kat, you just met him last night. Chill on the angsty teen movie quotes.

Shit, I'm calling myself the nickname he gave me now?

What the hell is wrong with me?

Okay, dude, you gotta get back to talking.

Right.

Alex

"What are you doing here?" I ask Kat, as if I didn't already know that she was here and that I didn't know why I was here.

It's been a rough morning.

Matt found me sprawled out over his hammock by 7 AM and I was woken up by a frozen margarita can thrown at my head. I fell out of the hammock spastically as Matt already started to talk about a girl who came to his door with something of mine, and my hazed hungover state immediately sparked into high alert as i remembered the events of last night.

"Was her name Kat?!" I groggily asked, running a hand through my damp hair.

"*Katherine,* yeah." He says, taking a seat beside me as soon as my body decides to jump up, my eyes widening.

"Why the f- Where is she?" I stumbled over my words like my legs struggling to stay steady as i ran to Matt's door.

"Damn, man. Don't act so eager." He says following me, shutting the front door. "She just had your ring, that's all." He narrowed his eyes. "Unless there's something else I should know about, because last time I checked, *bucko,* you were in a committed relationship."

I almost would have snorted at that if he wasn't so right. *Committed Relationship,* though? As if i didn't catch Felicia with-

Okay, dude, stop. You love her no matter what, right? This is just a ring. A ring you need to get back.

"Fine," I huffed, pretending I didn't care about the war on girl confusion taking place in my brain. "Where is it?"

"Oh, it went with her." He says nonchalantly, hopping up on his counter and putting all the empty margarita cans away.

"Why?" I furrowed my eyebrows and joined him on the polished furniture. "Why would you do that?"

He shrugged. "Because fate. I saw the way you looked at her. You were having fun." He says, emptying pink liquid into the sink. "And if it's meant to be, you'll find her." He grins maniacally. "Although, I'm not that evil. I'll give you a hint." He says, jumping off the counter and shoving a book in my face. "There's your hint."

"A book?" I looked at him like, *dude, seriously?*

"Yup." He said casually, going back to his backyard. "Have fun finding your soulmate!" He mumbled lowly, meaning for no one to hear but i certainly did. Loud and clear..

I am fucked.

But anyway, here I am.

"Oh, just reading this;" she gestured to her hardcover copy of *The Outsiders* as she spoke- "While I wait for my friend to get the right poetry book." Her brown eyes lit up like she remembered something and started to fish through the front pocket of her denim shorts. "It's weird you're here, I meant to give this back to you. Must have slipped in my pocket or something." She handed me the silver pinky ring back, an awkward tight-lipped smile painted on her face.

So that was it. Matt's foretold *"piece of fate"* was back in my hands.

Just before I was going to thank her, I heard her shrill voice from behind me.

"Alex, I've been looking all over for you." She says through gritted teeth, her eyes widening as soon as she saw Kat. I should have known, I can't go anywhere without Felicia following me, getting threatened by every girl I even say anything to. "Who's this bitch?"

Kat's eyes went wide. "Well aren't you a delight."

Felicia flipped her dyed red hair over her shoulder and did that fake-smile I've come to learn that girls do a lot when they're pissed.

Before she could open her mouth, I intervene as I see Kat's eyebrows furrowing and her lips curled in one of those smiles that say *I'm really weirded out right now and I'd rather be living in a igloo in Antarctica watching penguins have intimate relations than be here in this very moment.*

I swallowed harshly. "Kat, this is my girlfriend, Felicia. Felicia, this is the girl who found my ring last night, Kat." Throwing in little white lies to make sure you don't get a four hour ear splitting scream lecture never hurt anyone.

Why did I even slip that ring into her pocket? Was I under the delusion that a single person could represent the hope I had?

But I did it. I put that ring in her pocket, driven by nothing but trust in the universe and a peach wine cooler.

Kat

For the first time in my life, I listened to emotions rather than my mind, acting on complete impulse and not even psyching myself out by overthinking it. Like i always do.
Felicia, who Alex introduced me as his girlfriend, walked away and I never get in other people's business but I swear to God something wants me to care about Alex and get to know him better.

No, it wasn't because he noticed me at a party full of dozens of people and chose to talk to me- i don't need to be noticed. This isn't a 90s movie, I don't need to be recognized by a boy to feel validated and important. My self worth isn't based on the amount of boys take interest in me, let's get that straight.

No, it's because as soon as he was about to walk out behind her, I noticed his eyes screwing shut and the excessive amount of frizz he was applying to his hair by running his hands through them out of frustration.

I know that face. I've seen it on myself numerous times in the reflection of mirrors of public bathrooms as I would desperately try to wash away the anxiety and paranoia with cold water.
He was starting to panic.

Shit.

I'm not even good at consoling myself when I'm like this, what am I supposed to say to him? And why do I even feel drawn to the thought of helping him? It's pretty clear my instinctive skepticism of people doesn't apply to this person.

But, in a weird way, I saw myself in him for a split second. I've been feeling like I was alone my entire life. No one that i even remotely liked had the same problems as I did.

And, God, this guy seems like he really doesn't deserve the suffocating and intoxicating shit my mind goes through every day.

I took a strip of wintergreen gum out of my back pocket and used the pen strapped to the front desk to write my number on it, not giving myself time to overthink about him getting the wrong idea.

Before he could open the door, I tapped his shoulder and gave him the gum. "Here, this helps me when I'm like that too. Call me next time you feel like that, feeling alone fucking sucks."
He smiled weakly and mouthed a 'thank you' and walked away.

Did I just fuck this up? I totally fucked this up. It was so stupid of me to even assume he was having a panic attack.

Before my brain could take me any further, I told Ariel we needed to go. I needed to be home, in the safety of my bed, attempting to ignore the outside world again.

Somehow my stressed, over exhausted ass slept through the rest of the day, only to be woken by my phone vibrating against the wood of my bedside table. I rubbed my eyes and unlocked it to see four unread texts from a number that wasn't in my contacts.

It's Alex. Is this a proper text introduction? I don't know.

Anyway it's late. Kinda freaking out. Have no one here but my wigged out parents.

Call me maybe?

Can you believe I just realized that was a song title. Iconic song that shaped our generation, truly.

I chuckled to myself as I pressed the call button, anxiously waiting for him to pick up. "Heeeeeeeeeyyyyy....." His voice drawled out and I could almost picture his blue eyes darting around while thinking of something to say.

"Please don't start singing Carly Rae." I bit back a giggle reminiscent of Barney the dinosaur after five shots of tequila and squeezed my eyes shut in embarrassment.

"Not really in the mood." He said after he let out a light chuckle that i could tell was covering up his hoarse voice cracking, making me wonder if he'd been crying. I know that move. "Uh, can I pick you up? I just...." His voice trailed off. "I, um, need someone." I frowned at his ability to be somewhat open about his feelings to someone he just met, a skill I wish I had. My mind already threw me into a pool of anticipatory anxiety, something I've been used to for any time I went somewhere I didn't know about. Living in my mind just fucking rocks, doesn't it?

I took a deep breath, closing my eyes, remembering what Isaac had told me when he got here. I need to get out more if I even want to start thinking about getting better.

I do, and maybe little steps will get me there. "Uh...yeaaaaaaah." I dragged my answer out slowly, my mind still battling with me and threatening to give me a panic attack either way. "I'll text you my address."

"Swanky." He said before he hung up the phone. I'm not even going to bother googling what that means.

I open my closet to put on clothes that aren't pajamas, ultimately choosing the black shorts and plain white t-shirt i look best in. As I practically jog downstairs while texting him my address, I bump into a big, tall body.

"Where ya goin?" Isaac asks, blocking the doorway.

"That ring guy I was talking to invited me over" I say, gathering my things in my purple backpack. "And before you say anything, it's not a date. We just..." I found myself struggling to get words out as he texted me saying he was on his way. Why, god, why? "We have a lot in common."

"Ooooooohkayyyyyy." Isaac sighs and skips away. I roll my eyes and try to find my mom, but only find my dad sitting in the living room with a book in his hands.
Great.

Don't get me wrong, I love my dad- but panic disorders can be a hereditary thing and in my lucky case, Dad passed that shit down to me.

Which means, most of the time, he doesn't let me go out because of the circumstances it could leave me in. I'm usually fine with that because I hate parties and people and places I don't know anyway, but this time I actually want to do something.

By some miracle, he understood and only hit me with three questions (With who, Where did you meet him, How did you know he isn't a serial killer?) and then let me wait outside.

Miracle? Maybe.

Not long after I started picking at the blossoming dandelions on the front lawn, I saw a rusted lime-green jeep pull up in front of me, Alex waving behind the front wheel. I sucked in a breath and opened the passenger's seat door, immediately taking note that the whole car was filled with the strong scent of coffee and Pine Sol- not normal for a teenage boy, but I guess it's better than sweat, sex and beer. I sat down and he flashed me a smile, one that carried across his pink lips all the way up to his freckled cheeks in excitement.

"Whatcha doin there?" I furrowed my eyebrows and let out a chuckle, buckling in my seat belt.
"Nothin'," He sighs, pulling out of my drive way. "I guess I'm just happy I'm not gonna be alone with my thoughts on a saturday night for once."

You and me both, dude, I thought, looking out at the sun setting behind the passing trees, a smile of my own slowly rising upon my face. *You and me both.*

Alex

I can't take her back to my house.

First of all, my jesus crazed parents will probably be fighting over their lutheran and protestant roots again- like they couldn't just settle on christianity. My little sister, Jordyn, is probably home by now, sitting on the couch in front of their shouting and trying to mediate them. That kid's gonna be a lawyer. I should talk to her more.

Second, my sanctuary-also known as my bedroom- is a wreck. There are clothes and ikea parts everywhere, completed with a shattered window my lovely girlfriend threw a brick at.

I know what you're thinking. Long story short, she found another girls number in my phone that she did not recognize (my friend Emily) and got really possessive and thought I was cheating on her.

Emily is a lesbian.

I know, I know- Why do I stay if she gets crazy like this?

Well, we've been over that.

My crippling fear of being alone and without any familiar safety net.

And if I were in some disney channel movie, there would be a convenient rock in the middle of the woods that I could take all my friends to talk about nature and all that shit.

No. But, what I do know is that the library is quiet, has a sick space section, and has good coffee.

Thankfully, Kat hasn't asked me why I needed her company and about my girlfriend yet, which I greatly appreciate. We've just been talking about movies and bands- nothing suspicious. I'm already trying to reassure myself.

This is not a date, I say to myself in my mind. *You are not a cheater. Sure, she's pretty, but you don't even know her that well to be romantically attracted to her. You just need a friend who gets you.*

"You good?" Kat asks, stopping our conversation about Wes Anderson movies to notice me staring into space.

"Oh, uh, yeah." I answer rather smoothly as I pull into the library's parking lot. "Just feeling off. Let's distract ourselves."

"I'm down for that." She added and hopped out the car door, joining my side to walk in the double doors of the city's biggest library.

We settled at a wooden table painted silver on the second floor by the space books, The walls were painted a royal blue, with yellow-green star decals that glowed in contrast to the dark color. The dark paint made the room seem a lot smaller than it actually is, which was a cute spot in my opinion. There's also a big screen in the very back of the room, that displays footage of planets that NASA had captured over the years. Kat whisper yelled an exclamation of "ARE YOU SHITTING ME" before taking her phone out and rushing over to it, taking multiple pictures. In the little time that I knew her, she seemed very apathetic and guarded- it was nice to see her enthusiastic about something, even as simple as this.

I think that you truly begin to know a person when you find out what they're passionate about, what makes them excited as they talk and what makes their whole face radiate energy when it's mentioned. I smiled again, for what seemed like the 100th time that night, then even bigger when I realized that I wouldn't be smiling at all tonight if I didn't call her. I sat back down at the little table, waiting for her to come back from the classic fiction section up front.

My phone buzzed in my pocket, and my heart had dropped to my ass.

Yup, it was from Felicia.

I didn't even read it but I felt my leg starting to bounce up and down, and I started to feel my breath grow shallow- like I put a plastic bag over my head. Before it could get worse, thank God, Kat came back with a book in her hand.

"Dude, you okay?" She asked, furrowing her eyebrows and putting her book down.
'Yeah, just, um...." I stuttered. "You met my girlfriend before. S-She's probably really mad I'm out without her right now."

"I could go-"

"No, please don't," I rushed out, grabbing her arm before she could walk away. "I just...she doesn't get the shit I go through and I need to be with someone who does right now. And when you gave me that gum wrapper, you told me that feeling alone sucks, so I'm assuming you're going through similar rough shit that you don't deserve."

Her brown eyes softened. "Yeah...in fact I am," She let out a humorless chuckle. "And it's funny because it feels like no one sees how I'm just left with pile after pile of depression and anxiety on top of me, switching back and forth, and I'm left to wallow in complete loneliness because no one understands or is truly there for me."

My eyes widened at how much she was opening up to me. It was a little bit, but she was a pretty shy and private person, and she just confided in me. That made my heart feel a little warm.

And, I know exactly how she feels.

"I'm sorry I was talking about me and you needed help even though I won't even ask about your relationship because that's personal and-" She rambled on, and I put my hand on top of hers to stop her.

"You did help me." I looked into her eyes, smiling again when she let out a little sigh of relief. "We just proved every ugly thought in our heads wrong. Tonight, we're not alone."

Kat

After that bit of information we had shared with each other, Alex thought it would be best to get our minds off it, once he calmed down and promised me he'd stand his ground with Felicia if needed. We discussed mini golf, the incredible radness of Ruth Bader Ginsburg and of course our staples- books, bands and movies.

It seems as if his mouth can't keep up with his mind, so he talks a lot. And his sky-like eyes shine with little stars of excitement when he talks about the things that makes happy he's alive.

But I don't mind, if it's with the right person, I could talk forever about someone's interests, like now I know Alex only uses yellow golf balls, his playlist ranges from Bruno Mars to blink 182 and he loves to escape in the form of Tarantino movies.

"So, you read a lot?" He asked. "Thought you were a movie person."

"Oh, trust me, I am," I responded in mock defense. "Not every book becomes a movie though. And these stories have some very interesting advice about people that applies to life right now, i think."

He smiled and leaned his cheek in the palm of his hand. "Like?"

"Divisiveness."

"Divisiveness of what?"

"People," I answered simply, taking a deep breath. "In the past, present and future- one thing is for sure, people will be divided by stupid petty shit or strong moral beliefs, It's just the way it is." I paused, looking over at Alex as he furrowed his brows in perplexity. I sighed, and gave some examples."Like, I don't know, some people are capulets, some are montagues. Some are slytherins, some are gryffindors- but the point of those stories is not to base a person's worth on what they identify as."

He breathed in deeply and let out a "DAMN" almost way too loud for a library at 9 PM. "Do you get all of your life lessons from literature?"

"You say that like there's any other way." I laughed, scanning the back of The Great Gatsby, although I've read it twice before. "Besides the last two minutes of a Scrubs episode."

"You know Kat," Alex began, looking at me. "You've got some cool mind. And I truly think, someday, it will be too great for us mediocre humans."

I smiled at that, realizing he was quoting himself from the night we first talked.

"Thanks, dude." I nudged him. "Glad my mind could be of use when it's not conjuring up an existential crisis."

He snorted and draped his long, lanky arm over my shoulders and walked us out of our little moment and back into his jeep.

The ride back was quieter than the ride there.

He had informed me of the fact that while we're in the age of streaming music, he still makes mix cds. He reached in his glove compartment and grabbed 3 color coded cases and told me to pick a color. I pointed to the purple one and he smiled.

"Good choice," He said, putting the cd into the car radio. "'Tis funky."

I raised an eyebrow at him as Donatella by Lady Gaga started playing.

"What?" He asked, halting his dramatic singing and laughing. "Are you judging me?"

"Not at all."

"Are you *not* a Lady Gaga stan?" He looked at me like I had two heads, his blue eyes wide in disbelief.

"Please," I scoffed in mock hurt. "She's, like, one of my heroes. I just only dance when I'm alone."

"You're too cool to dance in front of me now?"

"Yup."

"One day, Kat," He chuckled, shaking his head as he pulled into my driveway. "One day I *will* see your crazy-ass dance moves."

I rolled my eyes and laughed at his white baseball dad language. "Yeah okay." I unbuckled my seatbelt and thanked him for the ride, getting out and watching him drive away with a smile so big my cheeks went sore.

And I swear, I haven't felt that simple little sensation in a while.

I went to sleep that night with a smile still painted on my face, spent the next day okay, saw my therapist, went to sleep okay, then woke up in a shaky mess of questioning life. My mind does that, I could be doing fine one day and the next I just wake up with anxiety, no damn reason that could even start it, it's just there. It's like as if each bad thought of mine is a vine and they're all tangling together in my brain, growing too high to reach the good things. It can happen when I'm doing nothing- *especially* when I'm doing nothing. People say to distract yourself with things, and they'll make you better- but how can you focus on drawing or watching your favorite movie when you have a ball of anxious thoughts tumbling in your head for *no* reason?

All that's in my mind right now is fear of my future and failure and feeling like I'm not even in my own body.

Fuck, I need to get out. It's like I need to let all of this anxiety out, but I'm too exhausted to have a panic attack. What the fuck is happening.

I checked the clock, only 12 PM and I've been feeling like shit for two hours with nothing to do, and I'm not even close to the end of the day, which just adds to me feeling empty with no sense of familiarity at the moment. Ariel left for her cruise, my parents are out shopping, and Anthony and Isaac are getting ready for their friend's bachelor party. It's not that I didn't have Alex, but we're still in the early stages of friendship and I don't want to annoy him, although it may be my only choice if I want to get out and forget my thoughts.

I texted him with shaky hands and one typo. As soon as I sent the message, my phone started vibrating with his contact name in bold letters flashing on the screen.

"Hey, what's wrong?" He asked, before I can even say 'hello.' I could tell his girlfriend was with him, I heard her high-pitched words behind his concerned voice. And I panicked.

"Oh, it's not-it's nothing, I'm okay-"

"Kat, you're stuttering," He sighs, softening his voice. "What's going on?"

"A lit- uh, a little bit of an anxiety attack." I took a deep breath, realizing all it took was a phone call to get all my anxiety unstuck from inside my brain and flowing into my breathing. I hate talking on the phone.

"I'll be right over." He says frantically, hanging up, making me feel bad that he's probably leaving his plans for me. Why? What the fuck makes me so special?

I've calmed down just enough to not continue to look like a maniac when he came, but my thoughts were still too loud to soften as he walked through my front door.

"Hey," he came over to where i was sitting, leaning against my dining room wall and assumed the i-have-given-up-on-my-miserable-life position next to me and nudged my shoulder. "What's going on?"

I let out a creepy ass laugh, like a snort with no humor behind it.

"Time," I said quietly, picking at my fingernails, turning them even more into tiny nubs. "I have none. I've spent my teenage years inside, being depressed and too paranoid about everything that I forgot to have fun. Sure, there's been good memories here and there, but the average day is gloomy and full of bad thoughts and it feels like I'm running out of time to leave my mark." I sighed, looking straight ahead, my eyes focused on a picture hanging on the wall of me at 14 years old, before my thoughts went bad. "And I've wasted the quote 'Best Years of my Life.'"

He sighed and turned to me. "Kat, listen to me," He says softly, putting his hands over mine to stop my picking. "You're seventeen. You have time to change your life. You have time to get in control of it, I promise you."

"But everyday I'm just nearing closer to my death bed and it feels like I'm doing nothing notable," I said awkwardly, trying to suppress tears. I fucking hate crying. And I fucking hate crying in front of people. There's another irrational fear of mine, vulnerability. The hits just keep coming, don't they? "I just wish I could age backwards because as I keep getting older it's not socially acceptable to be afraid of being alone and in need of comfort and reassurance, which I don't like to make it known, but I need all the time."

He furrowed his eyebrows and took a deep breath, "First of all, you're gonna be okay, I can tell you that. My mother may be a batshit crazy Jesus freak, but she told me that God or the universe or whatever you want to believe in wouldn't let you suffer for no reason." He put an arm around me, leaning his head on my shoulder, looking up at my ceiling. "Second, adults are human. Humans need comfort, Kat. You don't have to be a kid clinging on to a stuffed teddy bear in the dull glow of their nightlight to get it, and you don't have to feel ashamed that you feel like you want it."

We talked for a while on the floor, making me realize the cause for all of my breakdowns. It's always right after a good day. You see, feeling alive is a drug i get high like a comet on, and then i crash back down into the reality of my life- an endless stream of mediocre uneventful nothingness. The happy days are almost imaginary. The realness is boredom every single day til you're wishing for someone to kick you in the face just to make sure you can still feel something.

Yeah. That's me.

Alex

This past week was spent with Matt and Kat. Ha. That rhymes. They sound like a children's tv crime fighting duo with purple jumpsuits and capes.

I hung out with Kat almost every day this week, and we didn't really do much. Just complained together and mini golfed, and Matt came along with us twice, usually to remind me of Felicia.
Since the mini golf place is right down the road from me and Kat's already here, she's gonna try to drive there without freezing up and panicking.I know she's risking a panic attack, but it's good she has the courage to achieve a goal like this. I still don't know if or when I'm gonna break up with Felicia. She's been good to me this week, my romantic ass ogled over the effort she put in to engraving her initial on a ring for me and mine on hers, but I don't want to let Kat down. She's doing something she's always been afraid to do today, and in my mind it's only fair if I do something too.

But maybe not Felicia yet.

God, I'm weak. I tried talking to my dad about it, but while I was trying to have a heart to heart my mom was screaming at him from downstairs, making him pull at his black hair so hard he ended up saying that he would "shove her rosary beads up his ass."

Anyway, I still don't get why people put in effort on hanging around me, especially Kat. I mean, yeah, she has depression and anxiety and everything else in her mind weighing on her like a rock over her head but she still has the potential to hurl it to the side and do great things, I can hear it in the way she talks about movies. Me, I don't know what I'm even here for.

I jumped when I heard the door open, but it was just Kat getting into the front seat. Why do I let a 5'4" girl startle me.

"You good?" She asks, putting the keys in the ignition.

"No. You?"

"No." She takes a deep breath. "I don't know if I can back out."

"You can do this Kat," I said, trying to motivate her. "Just take a deep breath and relax. I'm literally right here next to you."

Suddenly, we heard another voice come from behind us.

"Yeah, Kat, you can do this!"

"Dad...what the fuck are you doing in my car?"

"Hiding from your mother." He says, looking frantically at the front lawn.

"That's healthy," I sighed, rolling my eyes. "Please get out now."

"Fine." He concedes, getting out the back door. "If your mother asks, I've left the country."

"As always."

Kat gave me her *what the fuck* look and I replied with a simple "don't ask."

I'd actually love to talk to someone about my dysfunctional family, but now, I really wanted to see Kat do this.

"Okay, okay." She shut her brown eyes tight and gripped the steering wheel so hard her knuckles turned white. "I can do this." With that, she took a deep breath and slowly backed us out of my driveway.

"See!" I smiled when I saw her face that was filled with astonishment and pride. "You made that driveway your bitch!"

"Holy shit!" She breathed, looking down at the breaks and her eyes going wide. "Oh my god, I'm actually driving."

"Hell yeah you are!" I turned on the playlist she made entitled *for happy times* to celebrate and make her feel relaxed. And after the first song by The Shins ended, we were at the mini golf place.

"Okay, just remember to slow down when you park." I told her calmly, but she winced and skidded into the first spot she saw, making us both lurch forward.

"Sorry." She cringed, looking at me apologetically. I laughed it off.

"It's okay," I unbuckled my seatbelt and turned to her. "Without some of the shit you do, I wouldn't know what being in a sitcom feels like."
"Hey!" She gasped in mock offense, punching my arm. "As long as I'm not Big Bang Theory."

"Nah," I said, opening the door to get out. "You're actually funny."

She snorted and followed me out to the entrance.

"Can't we just hop the fence?" She stops in her tracks and points to the gate. "It's not like we even do anything here anyway except laugh at unfortunate kids who get their golf balls stuck in the water, why should we pay?"

A smile grew on my face. If Kat and Matt didn't want to punch each other's shit out, they'd be great friends.

"Good idea." I said, looking around. The sun had just set, so no one is even really here. I could spot that god damn special succulent plant by the third hole and take it without anyone knowing.

It's like an inside joke. You had to be there. The thing is beautiful.

I perched my feet on the rod in the middle of the wired fence and pushed myself over, landing easily. That fence is cheap plastic and, like, 6 feet high.

Kat took a deep breath and followed suit, landing with no grace at all and wobbling in to a fake palm tree. "Okay," she says, dusting off her black ripped jeans, looking around the tropical-themed place. "What now?"

"We find the plant."

"Oh my christ," she rolled her eyes. "Are you still on that?"

"Yup." I smiled, running my way towards hole 3. Hole 3 was grassy and had a wooden arch above it, and at the end of that wooden arch was that pretty little succulent plant in a clay pot.

One problem. I looked at hole 5, that was in my peripheral from where I was standing, and a janitor was sweeping up the grass. Why? I don't know. But he definitely saw me.

So if we're gonna do this, we have to be fast.

"You really gonna steal this?" Kat looked down at the small plant, her thick brows knitted together, making lines erupt on her forehead out of confusion.

"Yeah, dude." I say, keeping my gaze fixed on the janitor. "Be ready to run, this guy is probably gonna be pissed."

"The janitor?"

"Yeah."

"Jesus christ." She sighed. I kept my eyes on the janitor and picked the pot up. His brown eyes narrowed to the point where they were staring into my soul.

"Should have taken better care of these plants, buddy!" I yelled at him before running to the fence, pot in hand and Kat by my side, running even a little faster than I was. By the mischievous smile lit up on her face, I could tell she really was enjoying this. Not long after that, we began hearing his feet not far behind me. We ran through a kid's birthday party, knocking over a few balloon stands to try and change the path. Soon we made it to the fence, and I tossed her the plant. She took it and jumped over the fence, landing without a scratch that time, and I followed after her, running down the street to my car.

"I'll be calling the cops!" The janitor yelled, still running behind us.

"Over a plant?" Kat shouted, sliding over the hood of the car and tripping a bit. "Grow another one to shove up your ass!"

I laughed loudly as I opened the car door and got in, putting the keys in the ignition, driving off to the sound of us giggling like kids in disbelief.

That was before tonight. Tonight, the night after the plant incident. Saturday at 8 pm.

Tonight, when I had my first breakdown that I had in awhile. I was shaking and on the verge of crying, but for some reason, I feel too numb to let tears come out. I don't even know what started this, I just needed to call Kat.

Wait. I do. It's Felicia. Isn't it always her? I can't stop thinking about her and yet she's the last thing I *want* to think about. She's the reason for all of my doubts. Before her, I was this confident guy and...fuck. She makes me feel alone. Isn't that funny? The person who makes you feel the most alone and most unimportant is the person who is supposed to love and support you.

After I admitted that to myself, I took a deep breath and dialed Kat's number. She sounded worried by my frantic tone and told me she would be right over, (she just got a new bike and she's been itching to ride it) probably thinking about having to sneak in through my window. I knew this because after five minutes she threw her boot up through the shattered glass and it hit my shoulder, telling me she was here, and I smiled a bit. I looked down at her, wiping the red from my eyes and trying to hold it together to make fun of this lame ass situation.

"Come through the door, Romeo!" I whisper shouted, leaning my head in my palm and waiting for her response.

"Oh, shut up, Claire Danes." She whispered back, walking towards the door. "I was going for dramatic flair."

She tiptoed up the stairs and I was impressed by how stealthy her awkward short limbs could be. She creaked my door open slowly and walked in and let out a breath of relief.

"What's wrong?"

Kat

"What's wrong?" I asked, picking up my boot that landed beside his bed and lacing it back up.

"I don't even know, Kat." He breathed out, his voice nearly above a whisper. He sank down against his white-colored wall and sat with his head in his right hand, pulling at his blonde curls.

"You don't understand," Alex says, getting up from his position. "Or at least i hope you don't," He winced, letting out a humorless chuckle. "What it's like to feel so alone when there are so many people around you but you don't want to say anything about how you truly feel because you already feel like enough of a burden and that's why the people who are supposed to love you act like they have something against you." He shakes his head, tears starting to form in his and my eyes. "I feel so alone here. The very people who surround me make me feel invisible." He starts again, walking over to the same window i threw my boot at to get in here. "The best part is, my parents don't even fucking know. And they're supposed to know me best, right?" A tear started rolling down his cheek and he frantically wiped it away. "No one could give less of a shit about me."

"Fuck, no, Alex, that's not true." I rushed out, trying to console him.

"I know... I know." He lowers his voice, sitting back down on his bed, the white, thick sheets matching the color of his knuckles as he clenched them in his fists.

"Its just...what do you do...." he mumbles lowly, shaking his head. "What do you fucking do when the person who said they love you over and over again is living proof that no one fucking cares about you." His voice cracks and another tear came rolling down the plane of his cheeks. I've never been good at comforting people but, god, how I wish i could give him everything I could because someone with such good intentions as him does not deserve to feel the same way that I do. I've found that depression works like that. It preys on the most beautiful, fun, outgoing people you knew, and toys with them so everyone can see if they're strong enough to stay that way. And most people, most people don't come out that way. They come out the opposite. Numb to everything. Cynical about everything. Living but not alive. Dead with a beating heart. Feeling like everyone is watching the sunset at the shitty beach, and you're watching too, but waiting for the waves of thought behind your brain to wade to the front, crashing over and soaking your thoughts in salty toxins while everyone around you is splashing happily in the clear water. That's what the combo of OCD anxiety and depression is. That's what it's doing to me. And I can't let Alex, someone as amazing as him, going down the same road as me. He deserves better.

"I just..." He looks up at me while a tear rolls out of his a eyes and down on to his wooden floor. "Want the company I feel like i deserve."

Even though I hated the feeling of hugging, i pulled him into my arms in that exact moment. I knew he needed someone.

He silently thanked me as he opened the window facing his roof, and gestured for me to climb out and join him. And we just sat there, quietly, making me starting to think that maybe I'm not as bad as I think I am.

Maybe I need someone too. And maybe, just maybe, he's that someone.

But somewhere in the tears glossing over his deep blue eyes, the stars above us, and the rumbling sound of the busy city made me realize something.

I don't deserve this. I don't deserve the crippling fear that something terrible is going to happen every day of my life. I don't deserve the obsessive thoughts constantly keeping me up at night. If I think that Alex deserves none of this, which he doesn't, then why do I? He obviously sees something good in me. I'm worth more than just a mess of depression and anxiety. I don't deserve all of this shit that I am going through, and I'm going to fucking beat it.

I'm taking ownership of my mind. I can't die with the dark side of my mind winning.

This can't be our forever. There is no way that I will let this take over my fucking life anymore.

I'm going to be okay.

He's going to be okay.

We won't let our problems have control of us anymore. "Were gonna be okay, Alex." I said out loud, wiping tears of my own. "We're gonna live the life we fucking deserve." I told him and a smile grew on his lips. "And we're gonna live like goddamn champions."

I woke up on a floor that wasn't mine.

I jolted upright, looking around. My breathing slowed when I saw Alex, sleeping peacefully beside me.

When did we fall asleep? When did we even come inside?

Oh shit.

I looked at my phone. Ten missed calls from my dad.

And 498 texts from both Anthony and Isaac combined.

I quickly dialed my dad's number and rushed out explanations and apologies in the midst of him freaking out.

"I'm just glad you're okay." He said once he calmed down. "I thought you joined a fucking cult or something."

"What the fuck, dad?"

"WELL WHAT AM I SUPPOSED TO THINK?"

"That I just crashed at a friends house who doesn't have any trace of satanic tendencies!" I whisper yelled. I can't really get mad at him, he gets paranoid and jumps to crazy conclusions all the time. He just wants everyone and everything to be okay.

"Okay, okay." He sighs, taking a long pause. "Is it the guy?"

"Yes, and I thought we already established how I feel about dating, so it's not anything-"

"Okay good." He whistled, like a load was lifted off his chest. "Just as long as he's not a prostitute. Love you. Bye." He hung up and left me confused. I decided it would be best if I just went home and talked to my dad before he thought himself to death. That was progress, though. He didn't ask too many irrational questions.

I texted Anthony and Isaac back, making sure they knew I was okay, and woke up Alex, who is probably the heaviest sleeper on earth. I nudged him with my foot and he kept snoring. I started to cover him with pillows and his eyes remained shut. I groaned really loudly and he just rolled over, knocking all of the pillows off of him.

So, it came to leaving a note. I grabbed a pen off of his nightstand and a post it note, writing that I had to go home and stuck it to his forehead.

It was surprisingly easy to get out of his house. His parents were arguing so loud, they didn't hear me open and close the front door. Luckily, my bike was still hidden behind the SUV in the parking lot. I hopped on it, pondering everything I said the night before, wanting to believe myself.

"I'm gonna be okay." I said out loud to myself and the sun and the surrounding trees, and whatever nosy moms watering their plants that might have been listening as I pull up in front of my house.

As I laid down on my bed and looked up at the ceiling painted white, I realized how much I've thought that in the past few hours. God, I must sound annoying. But, for the first time in awhile, I'm fine sitting here alone with my thoughts. Alone with all the infinite possibilities and circumstances of space and time and questions I'll remain with, because I'll be okay.

I can't believe I just said that.

Alex

I woke up peeling a post-it note off my forehead.

Gone Home, it said in the rushed, jagged writing I could only assume belonged to Kat.

Oh yeah. Kat was here last night. And her electric words are still left buzzing across my mind.

Everything she said was so right, so fitting- but how do we live like that? We don't really have anything to do. Our lives are so different yet so similar, we both want more but can't find any way to get it.

I thought back to those lists we made. Would we really be able to ever pull that off? To do everything on there, top to bottom, not just fantasize about it?

I think I need to call Kat again.

Since when did I become so dependant on someone I met a couple weeks ago? Before I met her I didn't even think about improving my life and all that shit.

I walked downstairs with my laptop in hand, sitting down on the living room sofa to avoid my parents arguing over who left the hose on, and opened the word document including the list I made.

Things Alex Needs To Do Or Else He Will Probably Drop Dead -

    1) Break up with felicia ?????

I scoffed at the question marks I put next to that one. Typical. For some reason, the impact of what Kat had said last night still left a bit of confidence in me, and I erased the excessive five question marks from the list. And fixed the punctuation. Kat is really rubbing off on me. Shit.

Things Alex Needs To Do Or Else He Will Probably Drop Dead -

    1) Break up with Felicia
    2) Crash a birthday party
    3) Write an actual song, start to finish
    4) Travel outside of New York
    5) Visit my family in Montauk
    6) Learn how to do something
    7) Find actual love
    8) Get lost somewhere
    9) I don't know man. You just gotta do spontaneous shit that makes you feel like you're worth something.

Huh. I swore I wrote more than that.

I'm way too uncreative for this.

I quickly dialed Kat's number for the second time in 12 hours without even thinking twice.

"Hey."

"Good morning." I said, rubbing my temples. "Remind me again why I wanna break up with Felicia?"

"I don't know, maybe because her emotional abilities emulate something in a ziploc bag that would be sold to me by a man in hello kitty slippers behind a 7/11?"

I stifled a laugh. "Kat-"

"You can do this." She said, taking a deep breath. "It's for you. And you're always thinking of other people. Put yourself first for once."

"That's gonna be hard."

"We can bullshit again today if you want."

I thought about this. It is about time I do something for myself, but this is gonna be hard. I don't know how to hurt people for my own benefit the right way.

"Yeah." I said, not caring that I may be getting too dependant on this girl. "I'm gonna need help with this."

How is this even gonna happen? The thought of doing it face-to-face makes me want to crawl inside myself.

I sat on my front porch for twenty minutes before she came into view, on her bike, in full black ensemble. She had her leather jacket from the night we met on, and ripped black jeans.

In june.

"What the fuck are you wearing?"

"I don't know." She says, getting off her bike and sitting next to me. "If I'm grabbing life by the tits, I gotta look like it."

"It's june."

"Do you see me sitting here judging your fashion choices, *bro?*"
"Uh, no."

"Thank you." She said, standing up and leaning on my front door. "I am actually sweating in places I didn't know could perspire though."

"TMI." I laughed at her, walking around to the backyard and motioning her to follow me.

"TMI?" She repeated in disbelief, furrowing her eyebrows. "Are we in 2009? Is that a Verizon RZR in your pocket? Did you download the new The Lonely Island album on it?"

"Shut the fuck up," I grossly giggled, nudging her arm and sitting down under the pine tree completely covered in moss and green caterpillars, the sun leaking through the pines and turning my vision white.

"What's this?"

"My idea tree."

Her eyebrows arched and her eyes got wide as she started opening her mouth to say something.

"DONTMAKEFUNOFME." I stopped her. "It works! Every time I've ever needed to brainstorm, I sat under this tree and something came to me."
She chuckled and sat down next to me, picking at the grass. "You know, you're the human embodiment of a disney channel original movie."

"Trust me Kat," I repositioned myself so I was looking right at her. "I know."

Kat

We spent the next half hour discussing how Alex should end things with Felicia successfully. As we brainstormed, we noticed that we normally handle adrenaline-rising situations by doing them and then running away before a consequence could arise.

Which is exactly what we are going to do right now.

There is another party at Matt's house, and Felicia is guaranteed to be there, and that means I'm guaranteed to have a panic attack. But Isaac made a harsh truth today, that I rarely ever do things for other people, let alone myself, because I let my anxiety get in the way and I don't want to be that person. Normally, what he says to me goes through one ear and out the other because it's normally utter fake deep nonsense, but that one stuck with me.

He also says I need to be more in tune with other people's feelings and understand them more. So, I'll have to work on that another day.

My dad actually encouraged me to go to this party to because he wishes he could help a friend out, but no one ever asks him because he loses it under the slightest amount of pressure. One time, he had to order food for a whole table and he flipped all the appetizer dishes and ran straight out the door.

Alex put on his dad's leather jacket and we headed towards Matt's house. We had essentially no time to prepare, so of course, it's starting to get hard to breathe.

"Hey, hey, you okay?" Alex unintentionally rhymed, looking over at me from the driver's seat.

"Just the fact that it's a party and I'm anticipating it with no preparation and it's fucking me up."

We pulled in front of Matt's house, and he unbuckled his seatbelt and turned towards me.

"You don't have to come in if you don't want to."

I felt really bad. "No, I told you I'm gonna be there for you, so I'm gonna."

"Katherine the noble." He chuckled, patting my shoulder. "Just stick by me and if you need to go, we'll go, I promise."

We walked into the house and the smell of booze hit me like a train. Shitty EDM music was blasting on the home stereo so loud that I could feel my pulse in my ears. My entire body felt like it was vibrating and the signs were set up for a panic attack.

Alex motioned for me to follow him outside, where Felicia was, holding a foam cup of something purple and doing smoke tricks. Fuckin' lame.

Maybe this is actually gonna happen, you know. I have a feeling I'm gonna walk out of this party, calmed down, proud of myself and him.

Our champion life begins in leather jackets and disposing of shitty relationships.

Alex

I can't tell if the molecules running through my veins and making my heart race is adrenaline or anxiety or a mix of both, but even with my head fuzzy, I'm determined to get this done and feel free.

I look over my shoulder at Kat, who is leaning against the back door, talking to Matt who is probably trying to be funny, judging by her deadpan emotionally dead face.

Take a deep breath, Alex. You got this. You don't want to end up like your wack ass parents.

Felicia surprisingly walks up to me, downing her huge cup. "Whatya doin here?"

"Uh, Felicia..." I say softly, as if I was too scared to raise my voice an octave. "We need to talk."

"Here he goes," She rolls her eyes, while Meghan and her other brainless army of droids who don't know how to blend their contour swarm around her. "Another overdramatic declaration of his emotions, although he won't even listen to mine."

Everyone around her snickered and fist bumped while my eyes grew narrower. "Actually," I began, my voice harsher than before, as if an entire hurricane of repressed frustration was gusting up the back of my throat. "That's the thing. You say I don't love you, but I do. It's you who doesn't, and I'm fed the fuck up with being your punching bag for whatever issues you're going through. Take care of them yourself. I'm better than this." I paused, judging the vibe for a second. "Who knows, maybe even *you're* better than this and all of this is just a dumb act, but as of right now, you are nothing but an emotionally manipulative stone cold self-righteous bitch and I should have realized that months ago." I took a deep breath before I realized I was steps away from getting in her face. Those words spilled out of me so easily, like Dwayne "The Rock" Johnson came here personally just to lift the weight of those words off my chest like, *Hey, Alex, I got you bro.*

"Goodbye." I said in a more hushed tone than my rant, backing away and patting Kat on the shoulder and running out to the car without looking back to see Felicia's fake face. Matt followed us, jumping up and down on his front lawn, a smile stuck on both of their faces.

"DUDE, that was unreal!" He ran his hands through his fluffy space hair, looking amazed and I felt a push of pride inside of me. I really did that. I finally did it.

"Yeah, you pretty much ended her," Kat added out of breath, only her expression melted from happy to get-the-f-out-of-here when we spotted Felicia's bad dye job squeezing her way towards us. "Run. Deal with this later."

So we did. Straight to my trusty Jeep, and away from the party. And yeah, the fire of adrenaline in my veins was just starting to burn

Kat

"Where have you been?" I was greeted by an interrogative Isaac at the door.

"I was out helping Alex with his shit." I answered, taking my jacket off and hanging it across a chair in the dining room, feeling relieved as the breeze of the air conditioner hit my exposed skin. "He just broke up with his girlfriend at Matt's party."

"Nice." He says, bumping fists with me. "I'm glad to see you getting out, but your parents were looking for you. I had to cover for you, so, you owe me one."

I nodded and thanked him on my way upstairs. Despite the great feat that was just accomplished, things started to feel boring. I feel flat, almost as if the writer of my story doesn't know where to go from here. Wink. But, I'm sure by this point in time, you're thinking of putting this book down. Bare with me, dude.

The neon red numbers on my bedside glowed 11:11, and for the first time, I actually wished on something. I never believed in any superstitions, or even religion to an extent (due to my parents- my dad being a german atheist who read too much Nieztsche and my mom being raised italian catholic and then not giving a shit after I was baptized) but I wanted to make an effort to tell the universe that I never want my life to feel flat again. I want to feel as awesome as I did today, and when we stole the plant, and even when we just met. The universe has always failed me, in a way- so I think it owes me this.

I sound like a goddamn control freak, but what I have right now, what I'm doing- is good. I'm making progress. I just went to a damn party despite having anxiety about it. I stole a fucking plant. I DROVE. I know in my realist mind it's not possible but I want to hold on to this huge rainbow chunk of being alive forever.

I never want to feel flat again.

I'm never going to feel flat again.

If it's up to me and the universe, I think by the way things have been going, I am going to be okay. I am going to be happy, for the first time in a long time.

Things will be alright, and not because the universe owes me one, but because I am in control now.

I will make this week great. And this month. And maybe this year. And I know I'll have a lot of bad days, but I'm gonna hang on to the good ones. Or maybe even just the average ones, because I know that things are in my favor.
With that, I put down my pen and notebook and went to sleep.

I woke up to the sound of Ke$ha coming from outside my window.

I peered through the cracks in my white blinds and saw Anthony and Isaac filling a kiddy pool with a hose in the blinding morning sunlight. My confusion led me to opening the back door and going outside, barefoot, in a long t-shirt and spongebob pajama shorts.

"Oh, hey, Kat." Isaac greets casually. "Watcha doin?"

"Believe it or not, I came out here to ask you the same thing."

"We're creating something bigger than us." Anthony said, holding up a jar of lilac bath salts that still had the christmas tree shop price tag stuck on them.

"It's 9 AM." I replied, looking at their supplies quizzically. Packages of bath fizzles & salts were stacked atop a boombox, statically playing the hits of 2010.

"And? We had coffee." Isaac tells me matter-of-factly, shrugging his shoulders as he dumps pink-looking crystals into the plastic purple pool and watching the water sizzle and bubble over, accentuated by sharing a high-five with Anthony.

"You know, Kat, you should call your boyfriend over here, he'd probably appreciate this shit." Anthony says and I feel my heart drop to my stomach because I know exactly who he's talking about.

"He's not my boyfriend," I take a deep breath, cracking my knuckles. "You know I don't date, you know, people."

"Then why do you look all nervous?" Isaac asks.

"I will hold your head under that fizzy water til your throat explodes."

Isaac held his hands up in surrender and Anthony chuckled. "Threats are funny."

"Where the hell are my parents?" I realized while trying to change the subject, looking around inside the screen door.

"They said something about couples counseling." Isaac replied as he put the hose down, looking at me sympathetically.

"WHAT?" I practically shouted, probably waking up all the late risers on the block. Why wouldn't they tell me they were having trouble?

"They said it was nothing to worry about and that they'll be okay, just not to tell you. Shit. Sorry."

I would say that I can't believe them, but my parents really never do tell me anything.

You must have noticed their serious lack of plotline by now.

"You okay?" Anthony came over to me, both of us sitting down on the damp grass together.

"I guess," My eyebrows furrowed together as I pulled on a blade of grass, tearing the delicate strand of bright green in half and twisting it between my fingers. Such different circumstances happened from the course of last night and right now that I can feel myself being launched into what the internet likes to call, a Depersonalization Situation. When you feel yourself being pulled from the world and nothing feels real in a sense, it's hard to describe, but things like this are enough to send the world's most unprepared OCD kid drowning in it.

"You seem spaced out." Isaac says as he sat down beside us.

I snickered wryly. "I feel spaced out."

"That's okay," He said, putting an arm around me. "We can do something today. Get your mind off it."

I stared narrowly at the grass. "That sounds good."
Anthony stood up and extended a hand out to me,
pulling me up and the three of us walked inside.

The kitchen table was empty. Which was odd,
because my kitchen table is almost always
cluttered with every paper and pen and empty
water bottle you could imagine. The cherry round
slab of wood is always invisible under everything,
but now, I've seen it for the first time in a while.
Smooth and light. A sturdy, plain, regular table.

I sat down and could feel myself disassociating
from familiarity, even though I was sitting at my own
goddamn kitchen table.

"Okay, we need to get her out." I hear Isaac tell
Anthony. I look up to see them looking at me like I
have two heads.

"I'll be fine. Once I stop thinking about death"

"Okay, yeah, you're not fine." Anthony says,
wincing. "I should have never told you about the
couples therapy thing, I'm sorry if I triggered this."

"No, this comes at any time. Cause like, life is
unpredictable, but also fleeting, like, who knows if
i'll be on my fucking deathbed tomorrow?" I
squeeze my eyes shut, trying to get images of old

people dying and all that other shit out of my brain. What the hell could have started this? It doesn't help when I can't even identify a trigger because that just makes me feel even more of a helpless weirdo.

No. I'm not a helpless weirdo.

Cause you know who thinks like me? Alex. I'll call him.

"I'm gonna go call Alex," I tell them, running upstairs to my cell phone. I try not to think about how dependent I've become on the first person I've found that makes me feel better about myself and dial his number. He picks up with a yawn.

"Hey, I'm sorry if I woke you up, but I just need a distraction from myself today. Wanna cross something off our lists?" I lead with a run-on sentence. God, I sound pathetic. What happened to the girl in the leather jacket ready to grab life by the balls the other day? Something in me is hoping he does have plans because now I feel like wallowing in self loathing.

"Shit, Kat, I'm sorry. It's my sister's birthday so I gotta spend the day with The Brady Bunch. I'll be texting you though."

"Oh," I felt relieved but disappointed at the same time. This is exactly why I didn't want to get too vulnerable and close with someone. It's making me dependent and messing with my head. Maybe being a loner with occasional friends was better after all. "That's fine. Talk to you later."

How does something as simple as connecting with someone and making a friend mess with your head so much? You literally just come face to face with someone who is similar to you and all of a sudden you're looking at all of your flaws constantly, wondering if they see them too and then feeling absolutely pathetic for even thinking about that. Worrying if you're being too clingy or too detached. Worrying if you're going to freak them out. Worrying if you come on too strong or too apathetic. Worrying if you're even good enough for a friend.

Maybe 'cause it's not that simple. I mean, when you meet someone, all the algorithms of the universe and the stars in time have to be placed perfectly in order for you to be in the same place, and it takes all the sparks of courage and desire for human connection in each person to actually start to talk to each other. And then it takes every ounce of interesting things about you to have them keep talking to you. And that may last years, or weeks, or days. I hope Alex and I last years, but sometimes I psych myself out. Like this. I mean, who the fuck am I, Bill Nye?

Yeah. I need to calm down.

Maybe I will do something with Anthony and Isaac today. I open my closet and get a mango-scented bath bomb that I never used and smile to myself. Who the fuck knows what we're gonna be doing today.

Alex

How do I not have any nice clothes?

Why am I just now realizing I have the wardrobe of a 14 year old hipster skater boy trying to be edgy?

Why is this book getting boring if you're supposed to be reaching the climax?

I don't know.

I'll spare you. Let's jump ahead to where this story gets adequately interesting again.

So, I'm at this Italian restaurant, and my phone keeps buzzing faintly. It's hard to hear it over my uncle's conservative and misogynist abortion rant, but after he starts talking about the "illegals" and my thirtieth eye roll of the night I hear it beside me in the booth.

Felicia.

Goddammit.

I'd like to say I regret nothing about that awesome, liberating night, but the fact that it was over and done with so quickly leaves her to ask so many questions.

But, like, does she even deserve answers?

From: Felicia
Received 8:02 PM

What the fuck is wrong with you? You think you can just leave me like that? For who? That Kat bitch? You are fucking delusional. Some other girl is not going to reap the rewards of what I made. She wouldn't even like you if it weren't for me. I practically made you the man you are today and you leave me, just like that? God, you are SO going to die alone.

I furrowed my eyebrows and took a deep breath. I could feel my chest tightening and my hands starting to shake. Fuck. I am not going to have a panic attack here, in a place full of people, and especially not over her.

She's not worth this, I tell myself. *You're away from her now. She doesn't have power over your mind anymore. She never did. Only you do.*

"Alex?" Jordyn asked, looking at me with concern in her green eyes. "You okay?"

I cleared my throat. "Yeah. I'm just gonna go outside for a second." I got up from the table, the rest of my family not even noticing as I walked out the side door of the restaurant. It was a breezy night for the middle of June, the small winds tapping me on the face as soon as I stepped out.

I shouldn't let that text affect me. I'm done with her. That chapter of my life is over. So why am I letting this bother me?

I'm not gonna die alone. That's ridiculous. It's ridiculous that I'm even thinking about this. It's ridiculous that I even have to tell-

"Hey." I heard a voice behind me. I turn around to see a cop, in full uniform. Tall guy, with a weird mustache that looks like a brown rainbow for his mouth. "You holdin, young man?"

"Holding...holding what?" I stuttered, looking at him confused, and admittedly a little scared.

"Meth."

"No." I said, furrowing my eyebrows. "Why would I be holding meth, man, my hands are empty."

"It's a simple question, mister."

"I don't have any meth!" What the hell is happening right now?"

"Okay, good, because I want you to know, that if you had meth, I would not, absolutely not want any."

"That's....that's nice."

Just when I thought he would walk away, he gave me his card and told me to call him if I'm ever in trouble. Why the fuck does a cop have a business card?

I gotta tell Kat about this. I haven't talked to her in only a day but I do miss her alot. Maybe I've grown codependent. I know she's trying hard not to get dependant on me. I should tell her that I don't care. She makes me feel excited again. She makes me feel like I'm a little elementary school kid, climbing the monkey bars and goofing around at recess in the best way. I've never had that with someone. That feeling where just being with them could make you feel like you're back in a simpler, much more fun time. I know so much about her, and she knows so much about me, yet there's still so much to learn. I know it's wishful thinking but she may be the best friend I ever have, and I want to spend all the time i can with her. Screw the rules of people. I'll play by my own.

I walk back in the restaurant, where it's like my entire family didn't even realize I was gone.

Yeah. I'm gonna see what Kat is doing.

I go back out and the cop is gone. Weird.

Anyway, I'm gonna text her and completely ignore Felicia.

Should I call her?

No. Text. We both hate talking on the phone.

Hey Kat. I don't wanna deal with family. What are you doing right now? I sent, slumping down on the concrete sidewalk, leaning against the brick wall.

My phone vibrates in my pocket.

That was fast.

Nothing. Bored as usual. I went out with Anthony and Isaac today and learned some weird shit about them.

I chuckled to myself and asked her if she wanted to meet up, not even realizing I have no ride to go anywhere, considering I came with my family in my dad's car.

I'm not gonna steal it. Am I gonna steal it? Nah. I'm not gonna steal it.

I feel bad leaving Jordyn, too, It is her birthday and she has to spend it being surrounded by a hoard of blonde, blue-eyed demons.

And I walked back in again.

And they're not there.

So I walk back out again.

I caught my parents and Jordyn right before they got in the van, not at all shocked that my parents just assumed I was with them.

I just rolled my eyes and told them I'm taking a cab to a friend's house.

The cab pulled up in front of the curb about two minutes later.

I looked in the car to see Rachel in the driver's seat. Barista Rachel.

I got in and tapped her on the shoulder.

"Holy shit, Alex!" She turned around with a gasp. "What a coincidence!"

"You don't work at the cafe anymore?" I asked her as she typed Kat's address into the gps and started driving.

"No, boss was a jerk, so I quit." She said, chuckling a bit. "It was actually because of you that I quit."

"Because of me?"

"Yeah, because of you. The whole block knows you stood up to your girlfriend, golden boy." My eyes widened a bit. How did they know?

Oh yeah, because Felicia puts *everything* on social media.

"You're a courageous kid, you know." She says, pulling in to Kat's driveway. "And you'll inspire a whole lot more than just a block in Brooklyn one day."

"Thanks, Rachel." I smiled and got out. "Good luck with this gig."

As soon as she pulled away, a tall man who I could only presume as either Isaac or Anthony came running out the door with a phone to his ear and a cigarette in his other hand.

"What the hell do you mean Monica's gone?" He shouted, running a hand through his hair as his eyes landed on me and it took a minute for him to register who I was. He just gave me the keys to the door he just slammed and continued talking. I opened it up to find Kat sitting down at the table with either Anthony or Isaac, a map sprawled out in front of them paralleled between two laptops.

"This Alex?" The guy asked Kat and she nodded. "Hey, Alex. I'm Isaac. We're in a bit of trouble here."

"What happened?" I asked, sitting next to them.

"Monica got cold feet." Kat answered, taking the pen she was chewing on out of her mouth. "She's their friend's fiance, the couple that's supposed to get married in, like, two weeks." She marks something on the map and put the pen down. "No one knows where she went, and she's known to suffer from some pretty bad depressive episodes every now and then, so we're worried about her."

"Shit...I'm sorry." I look at Isaac, and he smiles sadly. "How can I help?"

"Abby will be over any minute. We'll get down to business then."

"Who's Abby?"

"Monica's fiance." Kat said, not looking up from her laptop. I sat next to her and looked at what she was typing. She was literally googling *Where do brides run away to?*

I furrowed my brows at her, and she gave me a look.

"Do you have any better suggestions for the google search bar, detective?"

"How did that happen? I was supposed to be making fun of you."

"Because I am not focusing on caring about that right now," she says, not looking up from the computer.

"Right." Suddenly, the front door flew open. In came a tall girl with her long sandy hair in braids and wearing glasses, crying her green eyes out.

So I'm guessing that's Abby. Isaac got up and gave her a tight hug, telling her that we're gonna find her and reassuring her that Monica loves her.

"Do you have any idea where she could be?" Kat asks her, pulling the map out again.

"She used to say if she would run away, she'd go back to Cape Cod, but I doubt she's there by now." Abby responds, blowing her nose into a crumpled tissue. "If she's even there! God, why would she do this?"

"You know her," Isaac consoles her, rubbing her shoulder and guiding her over to the sofa. "She gets anxious over big things like this and her fight or flight kicks in."

"You're right," She takes a deep breath and her sobs subside. "It's not that she doesn't love me, it's just that she's scared. I wish I can help her."

I winced a little. This couple is really tugging on my heart strings. Maybe cause my first attempt was bad.

"Kat and I could go find her." I said suddenly, Kat's eyes widening.

Abby jumps at the sound of my voice and turns to me. "I'm sorry, who are you?"

"Oh, I'm sorry, I'm Alex." I stick my hand out for her to shake, and she gives me a weird look, but shakes it anyway.

"How would we, what would, uh, why?" Kat lets out a nervous laugh, covering her forehead with her hand and trailing it down her face.

"You guys have that list, don't you?" Isaac jumps in. "All these things you wanna do."

"Yeah," Kat says, squinting at him, giving him the signature Kat™ look.

"Wouldn't this be a perfect opportunity to finally get the fuck out of Brooklyn!" Isaac declares, jumping up and down. "Find Monica, talk to her, and maybe on the way do all those things you wanna do!"

I looked at Kat. "You said we should live like champions, right?"

She groaned. "FINE. I'm in."

"When should we leave?" I asked, my heart already racing in excitement.

Isaac gave me a *look*. Goddamn, him and Kat are definitely related. "Uh, how's now sound?"

Kat

I'm currently packing a bag for a trip I learned about ten minutes ago to a place I've never been to before.

Who am I?

No, I can't stop to overthink this like I always do. It's just gonna ruin everything. Isaac was right, i just need to live.

I swing my backpack full of clothes and toiletries over my shoulder, the weight, forcing my back to get hunched over as I jog down the stairs.

Alex is back with his jeep and a duffel bag of his own.

"We'll cover for you guys." Anthony says, writing down the numbers of Alex's parents. "I'll tell them you're a friend of mine and if they're looking for you, you're over my house."

"Great." Alex says, his lips forming a thin line on his face. "Doesn't sound shady at all."

"You got any other ideas?"

Alex paused for a second. "Yeah, you're right."

"Please call us when you find Monica or for anything else you may need." Isaac says, putting my phone and a bunch of 50 dollar bills wrapped in a rubberband in my backpack. "And if you're not back in six days max, we're probably all going to jail."

"Don't be so dramatic." I say, confidently, like I never felt so sure of a thing I was about to do before. "We'll be back."

Abby wrapped her arms around me and Alex, and he gave me a look but happily hugged her back as I was patting her arm awkwardly, signaling me to hug her too.

"Thank you so much, you guys." She cried, looking at us both. "Oh, aren't you guys glowing with enthusiasm. Like little sunbeam kids. Our very own sunshine kid soft cloud dream team." She sighed, and I tried to understand what she was trying to say. "And, yes, these edibles *are* kicking in, Isaac."

There it is.

"So, uh, should we go, or does this feel too rushed and impulsive for anyone else?" I asked, knowing this part of our story will be fast and make zero sense at all.

"No, you're good." Isaac tells me, opening a ziplock full of green gummy bears and putting two in his mouth. "Your parents are on that couples retreat anyway, so, better get back before they do."

"Wait, what?" My parents are away on a vacation to help their relationship to god knows where and I'm learning about this NOW?

"Yeah, they're in Orlando." Isaac looks at me weirdly. "Oh, did we not tell you this?"

"Uh, no."

"Oops." He says, practically pushing us out the door. "Well that's my bad. You'll have time to think about it on the way to Mass. Bye, kids!"

So the door closed, the jeep door opened, and the sunbeam kids team was ready to live one moment at a time for once, like true fictional characters.

Alex

We pulled out of Kat's driveway at exactly 9:30 PM, not even thinking about what we're gonna do when we need to sleep.

We were exiting Brooklyn when I gave her the aux cord. "Your turn."

I was expecting some mellow indie rock but I jumped at the sound of loud punk rock.

"You like this stuff?" I asked her, surprised. I'm not knocking it, but I wouldn't expect someone as introverted as she is to like this kind of music.

"Yeah, I feel like I can relate to it." She says as she turns it down. "Obviously not all the rebellious fuck-you-mom stuff, but in the sense that there's not a lot of good outlets for anger, and especially when I get aggravated, all I wanna do is rant. These songs do it for me, and, it all comes back to not feeling so alone." She paused for a second. "Do I sound like a hot topic employee?"

"Little bit." I say, chuckling. "Although you're smarter than I was in my emo phase."

"Shut up." She punches me in the arm, and I raise my hands in surrender and she yells at me to keep my "stupid eyes on the road" as I swerve to avoid hitting a squirrel in the middle of the road.

"That's why you shouldn't punch me, dude." I tell her as I try to catch my breath. "Jesus, you're violent when it comes to defending your taste."

"Like you wouldn't be, La La Land."

"It was a GOOD movie with a timeless soundtrack!" I defended, knowing what I'm gonna play next.

She just snickered at me and handed over the aux cord. I kept one hand on the wheel, and the other I used to plug the cord into my phone and immediately the soundtrack came on.

"Wow. You had that ready." She says, gaping at me.

"I'm one petty bitch, man." It was silent for a moment. "You doin okay?"

"Yeah, I'm surprisingly fine right now." She says, taking a deep breath and locking her phone. "How about you?"

"I'm thinking about Mike Meyers in Cat in the Hat."

She almost jumped out of her seat. "DON'T EVEN GET ME STARTED."

I laughed at her, realizing we were entering manhattan.

We're taking a little detour.

"Going into Times Square is on your list, right?"

Kat

"Going into Times Square is on your list, right?"
Alex asks me, clearly trying to hide a smirk from
making its way onto his face.

"Yeah, why?"

"We're going!" He says like a giddy little kid,
jumping up and down in the driver's seat. "Get your
selfie camera ready. We'll be running into a lot of
dirty drunk spidermen."

I smiled as we pulled into a parking garage. He
pulled out a $20 and a $10 from his bag and gave it
to the tall attendant. The bright green jeep parked
between two monochromatic italian sports cars.

Alex looked at it when he got out and said that it's
"a metaphor for life." I'm not even gonna question
him.

"Times square is about two blocks away." He says
and I swing my backpack over my shoulder. "We
got this."

We walked through streets full of big stores and
laughter. Alex had started skipping on the concrete
and singing songs from *Wicked*, giving me two
minutes worth of quality video footage. Our giggles
were almost as loud as the taxi cabs and
motorcycles buzzing their way past our expedition.

As we got closer to the lights, the more people began to crowd around us. I took so many deep breaths, pushing all the potential of a time-ruining anxiety attack down my throat, and with shaking hands and fidgeting fingers, i walked straight into conquering my mind.

I walked through all the people and the noise, my eyes focusing on the lights in front of me and Alex's hand on my shoulder. Normally, I would shrug it off, but if I had to choose one trusty companion to be by my side this whole time, it would be him. I looked up at him, and he chuckled a bit, smiling really big.

"Look where you are." He said in a soft voice, nudging me gently in the arm. "You did it."

A genuine grin painted on my face, looking around with a new sense of belief in myself. I pointed to a short guy in blue and red spandex to the right of us. "And there's spiderman."

His face lit up. He took my hand, and we ran straight towards him. No words were even spoken as Alex took out his phone and took a picture of all three of us, and then we just ran. To where? I don't know. We just felt so free, running seemed fit.

Until you realize you're in a city with a bunch of people traveling in herds and you're bound to trip over one of them somehow.

And i did. Right on my nose in front of the disney store.

"Shit." I heard Alex say right behind me. He helped me up off the ground, and I felt a little bit lightheaded. "You okay?"

"Yeah." I said, feeling the cut on the bridge of my nose. We walked into the store so I can dig into my backpack and put a bandaid over it.

"Can we make fun of me now?" I asked, and we started laughing uncontrollably together, walking back to the parking garage.

"Dude, you literally face-planted." Alex says, wiping the tears away from his eyes. "And now with that band aid you especially look like Paris Hilton had another rough night."

I gasped and punched him in the shoulder, only making him laugh harder.

The walk back to the garage was shorter than expected. Alex made us stop in an ice cream shop for extremely overpriced milkshakes before we left. He was happy though, one hand on the steering wheel and the other holding a cup full of strawberry flavored blended ice cream and smiling along to the Lion King soundtrack blasting through the aux cord.

"What can we do now that's on your list?" I asked him, knowing I just accomplished something on mine.

"I don't know." He says, keeping his eyes on the road ahead, the ever-glowing lights of the city wading past us, creating peaceful imagery I wanted to stay in forever. "I kinda wanna talk about that great feat you just accomplished.

"Oh, stop it." I blushed, giggling a little bit. I giggle? Since when? "That was really fucking empowering, but I'm still having trouble believing in myself, so I don't think I could have done it without someone telling me I could. So thank you."

"You gave me the courage to break up with Felicia." He says, turning down the disney music. "I think we're a pretty good team. Sunbeam kid soft cloud dream team."

I gave him a confused look. "Is that what she said?"

He laughed, smiling brightly. "Yeah. When we get back, I think she needs to give me some of those gummies. Good stuff."

"If we find Monica and bring her back, I'm sure Abby would award her hero with as many organic weed edibles as he wants."

"Which reminds me, crashing a birthday party is on my list."

"Recreational marijuana use reminds you of children's birthday party?" I look at him, confused.

"Okay. not like that. I never said kids." He states, pointing his ringed pinky finger in my direction. "First of all, having a birthday party after the age of 12 is perfectly acceptable, and on that note, breaking into a child's birthday party and eating pot gummies when it's illegal is definitely ethically wrong in the same ways."

"Forgot you were a philosophy student."

"Really? Cause I'm always trying to remind people with my gifted wisdom."

"Yeah, right." I roll my eyes at him. "So where are we going next?"

"Look!" He says, pointing to the sign on my right, welcoming us into connecticut, and I just now realized it's midnight.

"Okay, the timing on that was crazy."

"We are in the happy part of the story, after all." He announces wistfully, resting his elbow on the window and propping his head up on his fist. I looked at him weird, but I felt content, too. Maybe it's just 'cause I'm tired. Or maybe it's because the streetlights lit everything we can see in a heavy gold, making me feel like I was invincible, feeling like a true hero with all of this determination running through my veins. And I look to my side, seeing another hero with all the defining features of his face wrapped in glowing gold light, I *know* for sure this time I'm not alone. I'm not hopeless. And he'll never be again. And I'll never be again.

We're doing it. We're claiming our minds back, step by step. If our minds are the unexplored moon, our will is Neil Armstrong, and we are making sure our flag is in there tight.

Because for the first time in a hell of a long time, just by driving on this long road, I feel like we are so free.

We are so *alive*.

Alex

Kat fell asleep at some point before we even got to Bridgeport. Seeing her asleep with her neck get all twisted and leaning against the window while her legs hang over the arm of the seat made me feel tired.

I didn't really know where to go or what to do from here, so I decided to search for the nearest hotel on the gps in my phone. I realized that I haven't even thought of Felicia this whole time, and she's made her way to the back of my mind. I've been waiting for this feeling for so long.I don't even care if she's with another guy already, or if she's doing miserable. She deserves to feel everything I felt when I was with her. I know that sounds harsh, but ever since I musetred up the courage to break up with her, I'm done letting people walk all over me.

I didn't like the way the car was silent without Kat awake. I felt bad waking her up, though. She had a big day. I decided to put on more La La Land songs when stopped at a red light until we got to a hotel. My phone kept buzzing, getting in the way of my gps, so I pulled over to put it on do not disturb. I checked to see who it was, and sure enough, Felicia was still trying to call me.

Fuck it.

I blocked her. I don't need to care about what she has to say anymore. I'm no longer her scapegoat, her backup- in fact, I never was. I've always been my own person, and as long as it took for me to recognize it, I'm glad I did. Even though it took me meeting Kat to wake up, though she did encourage me, she didn't save me. No one did. No one saved me except my own mind and instinct. For once, they didn't betray me. I'm free. And there's nothing she can do about it.

I smiled to myself as I started driving again. I truly did feel a sense of invincibility, and I didn't plan on wanting that to go away anytime soon.

Kat woke up when we heard an ambulance go by on the opposite side of the highway.

"What the fuck was that?" She says groggily, peaking out the window.

"That would be an ambulance."

"Oh." She settled down, resting her cheek on her hand again. "Right."

"I just blocked Felicia's number." I told her, feeling a bit proud of the small gesture. "She kept calling me and for the first time it's like I have no subconscious desire to hear what she has to say."

"About fucking time!" She smiled. "Thats a big step, though. I'm really glad you did that."

"Even though you're not into dating, I hope that if you do fall in love one day, you'll learn from me and not have to put up with the shit I did 'cause you were so blinded by your own need to have someone."

She nodded, looking out the window. "You think you'll ever fall in love ever again? Or has she ruined it?"

"Ruined it? Please." I tell her, laughing a little. "I'd never give her the power now to take away the love I find everywhere. The potential love I could find in any heart, any mind, any person. That's something that I'm not only proud of, but something that no one could ever take away from me."

Her face softened a bit, smiling at the things I said. "That's actually really deep. Do you label yourself? Like, sexuality wise? Because I feel like I can't." She sighed, changing her position in her seat and fidgeting with her fingers, telling me she's about to tell me something she never did before. "Like, I can't box what I feel yet 'cause I haven't started searching, but if you know what you are, that's a great place to be."

"I wish I got there. In every aspect." I pulled into a parking lot of a hotel with ancient athens style pillars lining the entrance, vines twirling down each one. I was actually very impressed with the architecture to look up and realize it was a Best Western. We took our bags out of the backseat and ventured in, the scent of new furniture and chlorine distracting me from how old the building looked. The door wasn't even automatic, like most hotels are. The desk was the center of the large room, painted grey with an elaborate chandelier hanging from the high ceiling. The floor was checkered black and white, giving off a weird vibe for a hotel.

"Yup. It's haunted." Kat says from behind me as we get in line to check in. "I googled haunted hotels in this area. Here's one of them."

"What?" I asked, looking back at her.

"This place is haunted." She says, tearing her phone away from her face. "It's probably an old building. That's why there's a weird vibe."

"Oh." I looked around, walking up to the receptionist. "Cool."

I showed the lady my driver's license and booked room 303. She gave me the key and we made our way to the elevator, but I stopped dead in my tracks when I saw one of those luggage carriers.

"Let's ride that." I say, running over to the stray device taunting me in the corner.

"Oh my fucking god." I hear her chuckle and her footsteps behind me. "Who's steering?"

"You have docs on, I'm wearing sneakers." I tell her, hopping on the end of the cart. "I could probably run a further distance."

She sat down cross legged on the black floor of the cart, rolling her eyes. "You're lucky I'm more lazy than I am competitive."

We rolled on our way to the elevator and got in without anyone looking at us. This hotel seemed like a ghost town at this point. Is that a bad sign?

The elevator stopped at the third floor where we immediately stepped out and ran through the hall, not even noticing we passed our room number until Kat told me. I sighed and rolled us back to our door, pulling out the key and clicking it in the slot.

"Do we take this in with us?" I asked, not ready to say goodbye to it.

"I think we gotta leave it out here." Kat said, getting out and dramatically putting her hand on my shoulder. "And then we'll ride it back down."

We walked in and Kat flicked on the light, illuminating the ivory-colored walls with the matching fluffy comforters on two twin sized wooden beds. There was a flat screen tv hung up across from them, with a dresser underneath. The windows were covered with olive green drapes with the orange streetlights leaking through the fabric. It was...cozy.

I set my bag down on the carpeted floor next to the bed and ripped all of the sheets back to check for bedbugs, a thing I learned from my neurotic mother. I told Kat to do the same, and she noted that it was really smart. Once the coast was clear, we scoped out the bathroom, putting all the mini bottles of shampoo and conditioner in our bags.

Once all that boring stuff was done, we went back to the luggage cart outside. Kat called steering it this time, so I brought the pillow from the room and laid down on it inside the cart.

We headed down the hall to the elevator, occasionally stopping with Kat getting pissed at me for shoving my phone camera in her face. She pressed the button to head down to the lobby, and I looked up from my phone, asking her if we should try ghost hunting.

"You think we can actually catch something?" She says, chuckling and furrowing her eyebrows at me, making that *Kat* face that she always does. We should have one of those obscure cable shows that follow us investigating the supernatural. The poster would be me riding a ghost like a fucking pony, and Kat would be below us, rolling her eyes and taking pictures of us. Shit. We could make SO much money off of this. Anyway.

"If we do, we'll be legends."

"Like that guy who found those bigfoot footprints only to have his sons say it was a prank literally right after he died?"

"You don't believe in bigfoot?"

"Did I say that?"

"It was implied." The elevator door dinged and she kicked the cart with her boot, sending me wheeling down the hall and the first time I heard her actually fucking *giggling,* chasing after me.

She jumped back on with impressive grace, taking us back to the corner where we found this little treasure.

Right next to the sea of gold luggage carts was the door to the pool, where, according to google, is the most haunted part of the hotel. I looked in, and there seemed to be no cameras in the room. What a safety hazard.

I guess that means we'll have to go in, right?

Kat rubbed her band-aid covered nose while she and I shared a look, and she clearly knew what I was thinking about. Her brown eyes darted around the hall, looking for someone around here to catch us. "GO," she says softly, but like, a whisper yell, and you *know* how urgent that tone of voice is. I stifled a giggle and opened the door slowly, running to the part furthest from the window. She followed suit, untying her boots and rolling up her light blue ripped jeans, insisting that she couldn't get her shoes wet. I called her a diva and she punched me in the arm.

"I have the overwhelming urge to jump in there." I say, eyeing the clear blue water being illuminated by the lights on the sides.

"Do it." She mumbled, as I took off my own shoes, sitting on the edge and dipping my feet in. I'm not *actually* gonna do it.

"What are you doing?" I asked her, since she hasn't looked up from her phone screen in a long time.

"I'm downloading a ghost radar app." She says, sitting down next to me. I laughed at her way of believing in little wacky things yet still retaining a cold hard exterior, her resting face unwavering; those thick eyebrows furrowed and her eyes squinting to see better.

"Smart."

"It's still loading." She rolls her eyes. "Pool wifi sucks. We need to take this into our own hands."

I took a deep breath. "GHOSTS!" I moderately shouted, making sure to keep it at a volume where no one outside can hear us. "WHERE YA AT?"

She chuckled and we eventually moved on from the ghost hunting when we realized we'd never catch anything with just two iphones.

There was a silence after, just the sound of the water sloshing around under our feet.

"Are you, um..." Kat started, then swallowed her thoughts down for a second. "Are you as scared of the inevitability of being flung into adulthood as I am?"

"I've been trying not to think about it." I tell her quietly, leaning back on my elbows, probably only just to regret this position later.

"Shit, I'm sorry, we don't have to-"

"No, I wanna talk about it." I say, looking at her. "It's the only way we'll get better, right?"

She nodded. "I don't even know how to deal with it. Just being flung into life with, like, zero preparation whatsoever. It's like, here's a diploma, congrats, you're on your own now!" She sighed, getting up and starting to walk back to where her shoes were. "Here I go, I'm about to get fake deep again." She paused, sighing then continuing her declaration. "Growing up is basically learning to swim only with those safety goggles and floaties on, only to one day be pushed off a boat leading nowhere without any of that familiar equipment, expecting to be able to breathe and to not let the goddamn waters of uncertainty fill your lungs."

I stared at her. Where did all that come from?

"First of all, that's deep, write it down." I walked over to her and tied my shoes back on. "I feel this way every day of my life. Like, fuck, it's june and I haven't even chosen a college yet." I opened the door that led to the gym, which was still open, so we could walk out of there and not get caught.

No one was in the broad room, but the news was still playing at a dim volume above a corner mirror. We sat down on those exercise bikes and halfheartedly pedaled while we talked about the world as we know it ending.

"What sucks is there's nothing we can do about it. We have to watch everything fly by right before our eyes while everyone is yelling at us to keep up."

"EXACTLY!" She shouts and bolts up from her seat, going back to pacing around the room in anxious fashion. "Sorry I brought this up, I was thinking about it this morning and it came back in my mind again for, like, no reason. Now I feel bad."

"No, it's okay, it's necessary for us to show depth so we don't become those characters no one gives a shit about, right?"

"Yeah!"

We walked back to the hotel room in silence. Our bodies flopped onto each bed in perfect sync, and we agreed that we should probably get some sleep so we can be in Cape Cod by tomorrow.

"Hey Alex?" Her voice spoke into the darkness.

"What's up?" I responded, not opening my eyes.

"I believe in bigfoot."

Kat

I woke up to the sun painting a bright white over my eyelids.

Well. We didn't close the curtains last night.

The clock tells me it's 9:16 AM.

The TV is still on, playing through Friends re-runs. I look over and Alex is still asleep, loud snores leaving his parted lips. I unwrapped the sun-tinted white sheets from around me and tried to walk quietly over to my bag. It hasn't really hit til now, that we're, like, really doing this. I'm really doing this.

I take my phone out to see three missed calls from Anthony and 20 texts from Ariel. I laughed and decided to ease Ariel's mind first, seeing as she went to my house and was greeted by Isaac telling her I ran away to Mexico. Isaac really, *really* doesn't understand how to use sarcasm.

I told her where I was and what I'm doing and who I'm with, and she instantly started to spam with more messages.

WHAT?

I'M SO PROUD OF YOU FOR DOING THIS BUT WHAT?

I KNEW ALEX WASN'T A CREEPER. WHAT A GOOD DUDE.

SEE YOU SHOULD LISTEN TO ME MORE

TALK TO ME LATER

LOVE YOU

OKAY I'M DONE NOW GO DO YOUR THING BABY

I chuckled to myself and dialed Anthony's number, walking over to the bathroom. He answered after three rings, like usual. He asked me where I was and what I did last night, and I told him about Times Square and he seemed happy. Three people have told me they were proud of me in the past 12 hours, and it feels weird. I mean, it does make me smile, but it feels like I've never done anything worth being proud of, but maybe that's just the way I think. I'm too caught up in my own self loathing. Gotta stop that.

I heard a loud groan and walked out of the bathroom to see Alex awake and looking really disappointed towards the kiss on TV.

"Ross and Rachel fucking sucked."

"I've been saying the same shit for years." I said, grabbing the remote and switching the channel to whatever the number 53 will bring us. "They kinda remind me of Ariel and Matt, though. Who knows where the fuck those two will end up."

"Hey!" He gasps, getting out of bed and slipping on the Homer Simpson slippers that i had *just* noticed. "I'm rooting for them. Matt's less moody when he's with her."

"Eh, true, as long as they're happy, I could care less."

"You mean you couldn't care less." He raised a brow at me. "Saying you could implies you actually really have the ability to care less."

"Okay, wow."

"Just pulled a Kat on ya!" He beamed, jumping off the bed and into the bathroom. "I'm gonna shower."

While he was in the bathroom, I got dressed, ran downstairs, because there's only free breakfast until 10 AM, and I made those shitty instant waffles and got two cups of caramel iced coffee. When I headed back, he was out and using my hair dryer.

"It gives me the soft curl!" He shouted over the noise, noting the expression on my face. I set the breakfast down while he unplugged the hair dryer and I hogged the mirror to do my eyebrows.

"Well that little brush is adorable." Alex inquired from behind me, leaning in near my face to look at the brush I was using to straighten out my eyebrows with.

"Would you like to try it?" I asked him, and he shrugged.

"Why not?" He said, raising it to his face and clearly being satisfied by the way the tiny hairs looked organized. "So where are we going now?"

"I have no idea." I sighed, packing up everything we took out. "I guess just heading towards Cape Cod?"

"Sounds like a plan." He says, swinging his bag over his shoulder and opening the door. We took the elevator down to the lobby and checked out, Alex still humming the elevator music when we walked out the revolving doors.

We showed each other new bands while we drove up the highway under the burning morning sun, indie rock music shadowing our every move. It felt like a movie, almost. Because I really did start to feel alive, like fictional characters do.

We drove for about an hour when we reached an empty beach. Now, we didn't stop to think there was a reason this beach was so empty, we just got excited to take a break for a bit and the fact that there was literally no one there. We parked near the two foot fence, stepping over it and laying out the yellow quilted blanket, that we found in the back of the jeep, out on the sand. The sun was high in the sky and the clouds looked as if they were painted over the semi-clear water (hey, better than New York) and I was content. I was actually taking pictures of Alex smiling really big while he was trying to make a sandcastle from scratch, when I heard the loudest noise I've ever heard in my life.

"GET OFF MY PROPERTY YOU FUCKING HAGS!" A shrill voice stabbed my ear drums, making me jump at least four feet and instinctively grabbing Alex to run. I didn't even look back to see who it belongs to, all I know is if you hear a southern-sounding voice scream, you fucking bolt. Why is there a woman with such a thick southern accent living in the coastal northeast? Where even are we?

I didn't have time to think about that over Alex's goofy ass thrill seeking giggles and the sound of my feet picking up and landing in the sand that were ringing in the ears. Why did we park so fucking far away? My breathing started to sound like a rusty lever before two security guards stopped us. Shit.

"I suppose you two are the meddlers that broke into Mrs. Hunter's property." The shorter, bald one

motioned to us, throwing his cigarette on the
ground and stomping on it. "You two been smokin'
the pot?"

I didn't know what to say, so I just looked at Alex,
who was digging through the pockets of his jeans.
What the fuck is he doing?

"Do you know this Man?" Alex shoved a card in his
face, and the taller one with hair took off his
sunglasses and leaned in to look.

"That's Benny the Bull. He's fuckin crazy," Short
one said.

"He'll fuck you up if you mess with anyone he's
close to. How you know him, son?"

"I'm.......close to him." Alex answered, and I almost
visibly slapped my palm to my face.

He nudged me, showing me three of his fingers,
then two fingers, and once he got down to one I
knew what we were doing. Our car was only about
ten feet away. We ran around the two guards on
their dumb segways and straight to the car. I turned
back while we were halfway to the car, and taller
one fell off while shorter one was now screaming at
him. I've truly been given a piece of that golden
luck recently.

I opened the car door, breathing heavily and got in the passenger's seat. As soon as Alex backed out, the security guards tried chasing after our car. We lost them in the woods somewhere, with Seven Nation Army by the White Stripes blaring through the car radio.

"What the fuck just happened?" I asked him, not being able to fathom the events that took place in the last twenty minutes.

"I have no. fucking. Idea." He said, too spaced out to be driving. "But that was fucking AMAZING! The meth cop was right!"

"The what?"

"Oh, right, I've never told you that story. Remind me to when I calm down." He told me, slapping the roof and singing along to the song while the adrenaline just hit me like a ton of bricks. I started breathing heavy, but like, in a good way, making me want to shout that how invincible I was out the window.

"AAAAAAAAHWEREINVINCIBLE!" I shouted in a fairly monotone voice to the trees on the back roads and no one in particular, but Alex decided to join in.

"YOU HEAR HER, BITCHES?" He rolled down his window in yet another fit of giggles. "WE ARE INVINCIBLE! SECURITY GUARDS HATE US!'

I laughed at him, at myself, at everything that just happened. And it felt good. I felt alive. I felt like someone lit a fire under my unproductive boring ass and was like, *Time to live, asshole!*

This story is, like, five minutes long with no resolution or plot, and not to mention borderline illegal and morally questioning, but I know I'm gonna be telling it to everyone.

Because this is just when I started to figure out that I'm not just another hit and miss. My life is starting to become eventful. I have stories to tell, and I'm becoming who I've wanted to be for so long. The light at the end of this tunnel is almost blinding, but it's so close I can practically grab it.

Alex

The next hour was soundtracked to a bunch of confused laughter and declarations of "I can't believe that happened!" In the middle of my telling of the story with the mustached cop that thought I had meth. Apparently, he's some sort of big deal. I'm gonna have to google him next time we pull over.

We reached a main road again, and hopped right into a little 3 PM traffic. I felt a little anxious to get there, but I am having a good time on the road with Kat. She gets antsy stuck in the car, too, constantly clicking her long fingers and changing her position in the passenger's seat. She even said that if we get on an empty road, she'll drive. My mind traces back to that day at the mini golf place, the day she drove for the first time, and how amazing we felt. It was only a week ago, but it feels so long ago. That night, that eventful night, is truly when we decided to change our lives. Our lives didn't change overnight, and they won't, we had to decide to live how we deserved, which is exactly what we're doing on this highway in the middle of the day. I'm proud of us.

I look over at her, and she has the window down, sticking her head out with her camera and video taping the trees and the cars and everything we pass by, while her brown hair highlighted by the sun whips in every direction. The moment was mystical, and calm, and content. Then I heard a cough, and a declaration of "FUCK! I think I just choked on air!"

I almost choked, too, while laughing at her freakout. I wonder if windpipe failure was on her list.

What a subtle segue.

"We should check off a list thing." I said, itching to do something again, despite the events of the afternoon.

"It's your turn," She reminded me, looking through the videos on her camera. "What do you wanna do?"

"What can we do?" I mumbled to myself, thinking of my list and the opportunities near to do them. "We can write a song."

She gave me the face. "About what?"

"About........the sun."

"Why?"

"Cause I can't think of anything else."

"The sun...is....is fun." The words slipped out of her mouth in complete monotone.

"Fuckin A-plus rhyming, Kat."

"Dude, I'd like to see you do better with no resources."

I thought for a moment as I watched the sun go into the clouds and I silently cursed at it. "I'm in an unrequited love with the sun."

"Is that a metaphor?"

"No. It literally just never stays out when I want it to."

She chuckled. "Now that I think about it, the sun really is like a clueless crush."

I took my sunglasses off. "That pretty, dumb bitch."

We drove up the highway in silence for a while until we realized we were in Massachusetts. Kat put on a song with a sharp, loud guitar and bouncy falsettos and it made me feel really amped up.

"Okay," I say, taking a deep breath, looking at the sign that says STATE FAIR: UP AHEAD. "We REALLY need to do something."

"Is that something rollercoasters?"

"Something we'll both probably be terrified of." I pulled in the parking lot, that was more like a field, of the fair.

"Alright." Kat says, putting money in her pocket and getting out of the car. "Let's do this."

It was only ten bucks for us both to get into the open field filled with kiosks and food vendors with a ferris wheel right in the middle. Not a rollercoaster, but a ferris wheel.

Good enough. We're both proven to be pretty uneasy with heights.

"Let's go conquer a fear." I say, taking her hand and pulling her towards the ferris wheel, getting in line for the next ride.

The woman in the ticket booth was completely asleep, her nametag that read DELFINA was crooked against her rainbow striped uniform. I looked around at the line forming behind us, and knocked on the window.

She jolted awake with an abrupt "SHIT," looking around and smiling pleasantly when she saw us. I asked for two tickets and she ripped them out of the printer with vivaciousness. She handed them to me with a smile and we walked over to the metal gate where there was no line.

Is that a bad sign?

No, Alex, we're not gonna worry about this. Chillax.

The moderator with a buzzcut let us into a pastel pink cart, and we sat on the red painted ledges across from each other. All of a sudden, the ride started and I could feel us moving upward. I looked over to Kat, who already pulled her camera out of her backpack and was already filming the view of the sky. Her black painted fingers were drumming on the surface of the button on it, showcasing some mild anxiousness.

"It's happening," I tell her, stating the obvious, trying to push down a little anxiety of my own. "We're goin' up."

"Yeah," She takes a deep breath, looking out the window at the sunset. "Focus on the sky, though, the orange hue is practically melting into the pink. It looks like a painting."

I looked up at the peach-filled clouds that seemed to be getting lower and lower as we got higher and higher. Something about it calmed my nerves, so much so that I started smiling a bit. Kat glanced over at me and smiled, too, turning her camera towards me, making me laugh like, *Whatcha doin?*

She snorted at me and turned the camera back to the window, when the ride suddenly stopped.

My eyes widened at the jolt, and Kat chuckled in disbelief. When she was done sounding like the joker, all she said was "We're fucked."

Kat

"We're fucked," was all I said when the ferris wheel stopped at the highest possible point. "This would happen to us."

"We shouldn't do that." Alex says, taking a deep breath. "You can't just fall into a pool of cynicism every time something goes wrong. Just...just chill."

I stayed silent, because I knew he was right.

"Hey," He looks directly into my eyes, right to my mind, like he always does. He took my hands in his, and if he were anyone else, I'd tell their touchy-feely ass to get out of my bubble. "We can't be up here forever. We'll get down eventually. Let's appreciate where we are for a second. I've only known you for a couple weeks but I know you well enough to learn that you never take time to see beauty in anything. Yes, we're stuck up here for a little bit, but look out the window at that sunset." I looked toward the window and smiled at the sun setting over the water, finding a little contentment in both the sky and his presence. I've never had someone that could make me feel better in a nanosecond, someone who could slow down the gloom fast tracked highway of my mind and make it seem like a beach, no waves crashing, everything slowing down in a calming way.

And for the first time, in my life, I think I've achieved genuine human connection. I have friends, I have family, but I've never had anyone so like me and so willing to be right by my side in all these journeys of self discovery. I've felt alone my whole life, and I realize now, that I was just waiting for the right person to come along. I'm not alone anymore. I've found the Huckleberry Finn i've wished for, and I can't wait to see where every adventure takes us.

"Hey, I love you." I blurted out, then immediately regretted the statement. His smile grew as the red on my cheeks did. "Oh, god, I didn't mean it like that, I've never said it to anyone before, as you can probably tell," I paused, covered my face in my hands, got myself together, and continued. "I meant like, I appreciate you as a person and your friendship and how you're always there for me. You're a....you're a good......a good One."

He just chuckled at me, standing up to sit beside me and drape his arm over my shoulder, nudging me. "I love you too, and like, not to be cheesy, but I have a feeling this friendship is gonna be the best thing that's ever happened to me."

I smiled at us, and the fact that I wasn't feeling so drained after an emotional moment, instead it felt nice. A nice feeling. Sometimes I have this feeling of utter loneliness and disconnection from everyone else, like realistically I know that a lot of people are here to support me and everything, but emotionally I feel like I'm on my own floating through a galaxy of complete nothingness. You can't even make yourself feel better, though, because the thought is a paradox onto itself. You just gotta let the feeling pass and hope that it doesn't hit you as hard next time. I used to think that there could be no feeling stronger than that one, that nothing can conquer it.

But right here, this moment, the two of us, we could. At least for now. And now is all i need.

The ride moving again snapped me out of my head. "We did it!" Alex jumps up, knocking his head on the metal ceiling in the process, but he's still smiling as he's rubbing his head while we come down.

We walked out, feeling dizzy and overwhelmed, but ultimately okay. Alex figured we should hit the road again, and after we grabbed two blue snow cones and one red balloon, we got in the car. The hours seemed to go so fast in the jeep, despite how exhausted we were.

I didn't realize I fell asleep until Alex shook me awake while we were in a drive thru line at a

Dunkin Donuts.

The lady looked at us weird when she handed us two iced coffees at 11 PM, but we were too tired to care. The good news was we were almost to Cape Cod, and Alex didn't want to stop. He figured we could crash at the hotel that Abby told us Monica was at. I looked over at him, and through the curls hanging in golden ringlets over his eyes, he looked shot. I even offered to drive, not even thinking about how exactly i'd do that, since we're on a foreign road- but he was determined to get there tonight.

He reached out to turn the radio dial upwards, breaking the awkward silence. It was an 80's hits station, and the cheesy songs picked up our mood a bit for an hour or so.

Then we reached it, and our GPS pinged.

Welcome to Cape Cod.

Welcome to the better half of your life. You made it.

You have reached your destination.

Alex

We pulled into The Clamshell Inn at approximately 12:30 AM. Monica knew someone was coming for her, Isaac said so on the phone, but I doubt she's expecting two barely-mobile kids beaten down by the heavy fist of sleep deprivation. I honestly don't know how I drove this far.

So, we decided to go down to room 212 in the morning. For now, we'll be staying in 213, coincidentally one room away. Guess Matt actually has something on this whole "Fate" theory.

We got our room key from yet another nice desk lady and headed to the elevator. We were way too tired to take the stairs one floor up.

The room looked out over the crystal moon-painted atlantic, covered with white curtains in the shape of mermaid's tales. I say cute. Kat says tacky. I say she has no taste, she says fuck off and flops down on the bed (once she finished checking for bedbugs).

We didn't even want to take time to take a shower, brush our teeth, or change into something more comfortable. We've been on and off the road for more than 12 hours and we were zombies.

"Hey Kat." I mumbled against my pillow.

"Yeah?" She mumbled against hers.

"We did it."

"Fuck yeah we did."

And then the both of us drifted off to sleep faster than we ever did.

We woke up to the sound of an ear-splitting fire alarm.

Kat woke up first, her disoriented state of sleepiness and shock sending her tripping over the bed and hitting her head on the floor, and the sound of her big ass brain hitting the wood underneath the carpet was enough to wake me up.

"What the hell is going on?" I ask her, quickly jumping out of bed and opening the door once I got the hint, not even giving her a chance to answer.

We ran down the hall to the door of the stairs, a tall woman with short blonde hair shooting out from the door next to us and running behind.

As we were running down the stairs, in a not so calm fashion, it clicked that the woman behind us, with the rolex watch clinking against the railing, is Monica.

We went out the emergency door into the surprisingly chill June morning, the sand between my toes instantaneously reminding me that I forgot to put on shoes.

Kat shrugged the sweatshirt that was tied around her waist over her shoulders and looked around the building to see what was going on. She looked like she was talking to someone, nodding her head, squinting her eyes, turning around and rolling them as she walked back to me.

"It was a drill." Was all she said before sticking her thumb and pointer finger up, turning her hand sideways and sticking it to her temple and making an explosion sound, pretending her fingers were an imaginary gun. I chuckled at her, thinking about how it would be our luck that we decided to come here, exhausted, on a morning that the hotel would do a fire drill.

"Excuse me," a slightly edged voice said from behind us. We turned around to see the woman who I assumed was Monica. She had on a black silk robe tied around her body, but pastel blue slippers in the shape of dolphins on her feet. Her hazel eyes looked at both of us quizzically, looking as if she was putting puzzle pieces together. "Are you guys Kat and Alex?"

"We are," I said, extending my hand. "You must be Monica."

"Pleasure to meet you, Alex, I presume." She says, shaking my hand and laughing awkwardly.

"Yeah, that's me," I tell her, looking behind me and wrapping my arm around Kat's shoulder, pulling her away from side-eyeing this couple giving the three of us weird looks. "This is Kat."

"Nice to meet you too!" Monica beamed, shaking Kat's hand now. "Anthony told me a lot about you."

Kat's eyebrows extended over the length of her forehead as she stammered for something to say. "Likewise!" She lied.

"Listen, we uh, we don't have to talk about this if you don't want to." I told her, trying to lead the elephant out of the room. "We're just here to take you home, safely, you know."

"Yeah, no shame in having breakdowns when you're with these kids." Kat added with her slightly awkward half smile she always has.

She blushed a little and smiled shyly. "Thank you guys," She says, walking back towards the building once the alarm stopped. "Can I at least get you guys breakfast here? The pancakes are amazing."

So we followed her and walked back inside, all of us in a line, leaving the sand and the peach-lit sunrise behind.

We entered the lobby, and it looked totally different from the way it did last night. The walls were a pale blue, and the furniture a bright yellow. Everything was of nautical theme, to the point where Kat was right- it *was* tacky. She led us down a hall from that room, to one with a wooden ceiling and stone walls. It had a bar in the middle, not like an alcoholic bar, but a bar with stools lining each side. There were other booths and tables throughout the room, and at the very back was what I can only guess was a mini travel-sized bakery. There were display cases full of croissants and donuts and a window at the back that looked into the kitchen. Monica ordered all of us a plate of pancakes and a cappuccino. We sat at the table nearest to the floor-to-ceiling windows, overlooking the beach and the sun finishing its rise.

Monica asked us what we did on the drive up here, and we explained in full enthusiastic detail the night we left, times square, our first hotel, the beach incident with "Benny the Bull", the ferris wheel and everything else. She seemed genuinely interested in our stories, her eyes looking into ours and smiling at our antics.

"How did you guys meet?" She asked us, starting on her pancakes.

Kat answered for me, something she normally doesn't do - showing that she has already grown comfortable with Monica. "We were both at a party we didn't want to be at." She says, finishing her coffee. "So we happened to be outside at the same time and we started talking, Alex here was a little slap-happy and dropped his pinky ring in my pocket, we bumped into each other again and I returned it, and we've been friends since."

"Sounds like the universe doing you a favor." She winked at us, excusing herself to the bathroom. Do her and Matt know each other

I looked at Kat and she shrugged, making me laugh. Once Monica came back, we went back to our rooms and got ready to leave.

She invited us in her room once we were checked out, and we sat on the two twin beds while she was doing her makeup in the bathroom. Kat scooted up in the center of the mattress, and watched her acid-wash denim covered legs swing aimlessly off the edge.

It's weird to sit here in the comfortable silence and realized that we did this, that we're actually here, this spontaneous trip is almost done, and I'll be graduating when I get back. What I didn't tell Kat was that I actually did apply to one school- the Eastman School of Music up in Rochester. I didn't tell anyone because there's not a good chance of me getting in - in my mind anyway - and I don't want to get anyone's hopes up. I don't need to start viewing myself as a failure again. I know it's not likely I'm getting in, but that's the only college I see myself going to. It's either Eastman or nothing. And if it's not Eastman, I hope my life is filled with days like these past ones- simple, yet undoubtedly alive.

Monica came out of the bathroom in an excited rush, obviously overcompensating for the reason we're here in the first place. I don't mind, though, I understand how much easier it is to conceal your problems with a charming smile and happy eyes. I don't think she'll end up talking to us about it, I'll be surprised if she does.

I asked her if her car is here, and she told us she came up here on the train. So, we got in my jeep, and she offered to drive, so I let her. Kat sat in the back, her legs taking up the whole row. I got in the passenger's seat because Kat didn't realize we were calling shotgun. On the way through Massachusetts, we showed Monica our spotify playlist entitled *We're Doing This* compiled of movie musical soundtracks, The White Stripes, The Black Keys, Weezer, Blink-182 and 70's-90's jams. She complimented our music taste, and said how "you could tell a lot about a person through what kind of songs they listen to." Her conclusion was that we were two very ambitious people who want to be badasses but are secret softies.

"Ding ding ding!" Kat said without looking up from her phone. Monica laughed and offered to get us food again around lunch time. If this section of our story seems rushed, it's because the day was a blur of not doing much, and for the first time for both of us, it was comforting.

We passed through Rhode Island in daylight this time, the national capital of contrast. We drove by beach side mansions one minute, then entered a trailer town the next. It's always baffled me. This state is like a portal to another dimension.

We stopped at a diner next to a rest stop off the highway, and the three of us got waffles again instead of pancakes this time. The diner was cute, it was 50's themed like many diners are. We sat there and talked about the best true crime shows and broadway musicals. The chocolate milkshake we all ordered made me devour what was left of Monica's TUMS roll. I've never taken one before, let alone two, so Kat informed me that they tasted like a stick of chalk fucked a Kit-Kat wafer. She was right.

By 3 in the afternoon we were back in Connecticut, our certified halfway point. We made it this far without hitting any traffic, which means it's creeping up on us soon.

We anticipated the oncoming traffic with road games, more specifically, making up a movie with each passing driver as a character; giving them a backstory and everything. Kat keeps making the old Italian guys mob bosses.

Monica was giving the old lady next to us superpowers when the traffic hit. "Time to go to sleep, kids." She announced, pausing the music and putting her headphones in. "You need it."

I turned around and Kat was already half asleep, her green army jacket bunched up in the space between her head and the window. It didn't take long before I dozed off either, because all of a sudden I woke up in upstate New York.

The sun was well on it's way to setting against a bright pink and blue 6 pm sky when I opened my eyes. Kat was already awake, her window rolled down and her camera sticking out of it. Monica had her bluetooth in her ear, having a conversation on the other end as she sipped at her coffee.

I turned back to Kat. "You want shotgun the next time we stop?"

"No," She says, her brown eyes never moving from their comfortable spot on the window. "I like it back here. It's roomy."

Monica hung up the phone a few minutes later. "That was Abby," she said, a nervousness creeping into her voice. "While you guys were sleeping, I talked to her about everything. She understands, and the wedding is still on."

"Oh I knew she would!" I said to her after an awkward pause, and I realized Kat probably isn't gonna say anything before I do. "Are you still nervous for the wedding?"

"Actually, no," She says with the prologue of a smile writing across her face. "After talking to her...I'm really excited. I'm ready to start our lives together."

"I'm really happy for you guys." Kat chimed in, taking the headphones out of her ears. "I'm not a big fan of marriage by any standards, but I'm a big fan of a person who is getting married because they *know* they'll be happy, not just for the hell of it like my parents did."

Monica laughed. "Thanks, kid."

We rode down to a Stew Leonard's because we started to get snacky, and what better to snack on then generic brand cashews in a tub surrounded by animatronic farm animals staring you down.

Kat got out of the car first, not knowing what she was about to encounter.

Kat

I look down and a chicken runs past me, just short of my feet.

Where am I?

A man in a black polo runs after it, almost tripping over Alex's untied shoelaces and clipping out a short "SORRY!"

I think I've entered another dimension.

Monica and Alex laugh hysterically as the three of us walk through the automatic doors into this gigantic store.

Immediately my eye caught a giant animatronic cow sitting on top of the grocery shelves playing a fiddle and I jumped. Alex just giggled wildly at me as he took a tub of chocolate cashews off of the shelf. Monica grabbed a red shopping cart from the corner and adjusted her glasses, furrowing her brows at the cow.

"Is this purgatory?" I ask her, and she laughs at me, taking her glasses off.

"If purgatory were to exist on God's green earth, there would be no reason for me to think that it wouldn't be in this All-American creepy ass grocery store."

Alex ran back to us, breathless, but clearly excited. "GUYS, THERE'S PUPPIES HERE."

What the fuck is this place?

He leads us through aisles and displays to the corner of the store with fish tanks lined up everywhere and, sure enough, a window looking into a room of puppies.

Puppies in stores always make me sad, knowing that they don't know a world outside of the glass. Dogs deserve so much better. I mean, they're not people. They don't know how to suck.

Monica and Alex were really happy about it, though. They were naming them, making them follow their fingers and already getting too attached through the glass.

I smiled at them and walked over to the bright blue fish tank near the employee's entrance, and let the neon fish calm me down. I always loved going to pet stores and looking at the fish since I was little; the colors of them and the way they move around are almost therapeutic. Maybe I need a fish.

I look at the price. Literally $5 a fish. What the fuck is this place. I rummage through the money in my jacket pocket and see if i have enough left for fish food and a tank. Thankfully, I don't- the universe just saved me from this impulse buy.

"Kat you ready to go?" Monica snapped me out of it, tossing me a bag of gummy worms that I assume are mine.

I took a subtle deep sigh, gliding back to reality. "Yeah, let's go."

We paid for and bagged our stuff and went out the door back into our normal universe.

"Hey Kat?" Alex said, opening the back door to the jeep, tossing me his keys. "What do you think about driving for a while?"

Can I do that? Can I really drive on a main road like that?

"I'll...I mean, I'll try." I said, walking over to the driver's seat.

"That's my girl!" He ruffles my hair, probably putting a further knot in it as he gets in the back. Monica gets in the passenger's seat beside me, and tells me that if I need her to drive, to just pull over on the side of the road where no cars are passing and let her take over.

I put the keys in the ignition and slowly pulled out of the parking lot, my breathing getting quicker as my pace remained slow. There weren't as many cars on the highway as I thought, at least not in the HOV lane. The more I drove, the more anxiety faded away. Alex was playing some calming indie music that went along with the sunset, and that was helping a lot.

We played the same road game as before, but my nerves didn't let me participate much; they just forced me to keep my mouth shut and my breathing steady and my eyes on the road because you don't know if you could kill everyone in here with one wrong move!

I do have to say, though, besides the subtle anxiety I didn't let Monica or Alex see, I am pretty proud of myself for doing this without a complete freakout. With their starry-eyed laughter cutting through silence beside the cosmic guitar licks of Mac DeMarco, it was almost...relaxing?

There was a rest-stop near Yonkers about a half hour later where I finally stopped and felt like I've reached my limit. Nighttime traffic was coming, and that was something I wasn't quite ready to deal with yet.

"I'll drive the way back," Alex said, getting out of the car and stretching. "I was getting too antsy back there."

As he's jogging in place, hitting his knees up to his hands and cracking his knuckles, Monica went and got us starbucks for the rest of the ride and I made my way into the back again. It's cozy there.

"You doin okay?" Alex asks me through the rolled down window, as he continues to stretch and not stand still.

"Yeah," I tell him with a smile, remembering how I could find the embodiment of warmth and friendship and safeness in just one friend and one month. Gross. But true. "You?"

"Yeah." He replied, getting in the driver's seat. "I'm oddly ready to get home."

Monica came out with a tray full of iced lattes and got in the back, handing us each a cup. I swear, I've consumed so much caffeine on this trip I feel like a rocketship.

I realized how we all completely changed our seats when Alex drove us back on the highway. The next two hours were full of us making small talk, Alex told us about how he doesn't even feel anything for Felicia anymore, and how he's so glad that he got that quote "shitwreck" out of his life. Monica asked us to come to her wedding, and told us about her bridesmaids (there's Audrey, Em, Hanna, Allison, Martie, Kayla and Melissa) and their matching dresses and how we'd probably need to sit with them. We hit a patch of traffic again, but we ultimately got back in Brooklyn around 8:30.

Alex dropped Monica off at her apartment first, and Abby came out to thank us, offering us pina coladas and a viewing of *The Room*, but we told her we needed to get back home.

As we pulled out of the parking garage, we saw them standing by the elevator, embracing each other in a tight hug. I smiled a little bit, knowing they're both in good hands.

"Is the concept of love selling you yet?" Alex asked, catching me smirking.

"Maybe a little bit," I rolled my eyes. "I've been around your cheesy ass way too much."

He laughed as he pulled into my driveway, with Anthony and Isaac on the porch waiting for us.

They jumped up and down obnoxiously when they saw us and quickly ran towards the car.

"HOW'D YOU DO HOW'D YOU DO HOW'D YOU DO" Isaac shouted as we got out and went around the back to get my bag.

"We, uh," Alex started, high-fiving both of them. "We had fun."

"What did you guys do?" Anthony said, ruffling my hair. "Anything illegal?"

"Maybe," I tell him, opening the door to inside of the house where both my parents are sitting at the dining table, looking right at me.

"Why didn't you tell me?" I whispered through my teeth towards Anthony and Isaac, who just looked at me apologetically, saying they wanted to savor my happiness.

"Your cousins told us everything," My mom started, getting up out of her chair and walking towards me. "And as pissed as I am that you didn't think once to tell me where you are, I'm glad it wasn't anything bad."

Even though her tone seemed civil, my jaw unhinged in disbelief and words I'd probably gonna regret would come pouring out any second. "Mom, you went on a couple's retreat with dad and I had to hear about it from Anthony!" I set my bag down and pinched the bridge of my nose, trying to seem less annoyed and caught off guard. "Look, I'm sorry I didn't tell you, but you didn't tell me where you were either!"

She took a deep breath, clearly trying not to yell. I assessed the situation for a nanosecond, never hearing my mother raise her voice before. My father walked over to her and held her arm, and my mind noted that that was the first time I've seen them touch in, like, a year. Maybe they needed that trip. Maybe they didn't tell me because they didn't want me to know they've been having problems.

"We didn't want you to know we were going through a rough patch," There it is. "We didn't want to put more stress on your shoulders than you already have."

"You don't have to worry about me."

"Clearly we do!" My mom shouted, then taking a quick deep breath to calm herself. "I'm pissed at you for not telling me, and you have every right to be pissed at me, but just know one thing- no matter what, your father and I are very proud of you for doing this."

"Hell, I would never have half the bravery you do," My dad started, making me smile. "And while you will never do this again, I'm so proud that you found the courage to battle your mind," He continued as he started to get teary eyed. "I'm still trying to, and I'm twenty five years older than you."

He pulled me in for a hug, and I reciprocated. I've been giving a lot of hugs lately. "Keep fighting those monsters in your mind," he says over my shoulder, holding me tight. "Just make sure we know what you're doing with them first."

Then my mom joined us, then Anthony and Isaac. As soon as I started to feel slightly claustrophobic, I peered over my dad's shoulder at Alex standing there, awkwardly looking at the wallpaper. I motioned for him to come over as I broke away, introducing my parents to him.

"Anthony and Isaac said you guys weren't dating and I trust them." My mom said as she extended her hand out towards him and I dropped my face in my palms, mumbling *Just friends mom, friends.* She started laughing, saying "I'm kidding, I'm kidding! I'm not that embarrassing!"

"It's nice to meet you Mrs. Rudnitsky. Kat told me a lot about you." Alex awkwardly lied as he shook her hand. "You as well, Mr. Rudnitsky. Nice to meet you."

"Likewise!" My dad says, bringing him into a hug. "Thank you for helping my daughter conquer her fears."

"Honestly, she helped me with mine too," Alex gestured towards me, smiling. "If I haven't met her, I'd still have an annoying girlfriend that was way too toxic for me," He paused, looking at me with a soft face. "Kat encouraged me to call it off with her, and so much more. I think, after these past few days, I've truly found a best friend for life in her."

I smiled at him, standing on my tippy toes to ruffle his hair like an annoying big brother would do. "Don't get all mushy on me, now."

"I can't help it, it's like we bought life in bulk in costco and truly indulged ourselves in it for only a few simple days riding in the car." Alex said, laughing a little and looking for his keys. "I'll leave you guys to it, I should be going."

"No, stay!" My mom grabs his arm, pulling him to the dining table. "We wanna hear all about this trip!"

"Oh, I don't wanna impose-"

"Trust me, you're not." My dad says, taking a seat at the table and grabbing the phone. "I'll order a pizza. I wanna talk about everything!"

Alex and I sat down with them, and spent an hour or so explaining how Monica ran away and we brought her back in search for spontaneity and doing things that scare us. It was around 10:30 when Alex decided to call it quits and head out the door, but not before making my parents laugh and tell them how much I've helped him, making my face red throughout the entirety of the conversation. Almost 18 years and I still don't know how to deal with praise like a functioning human adult.

I walked him out to his car, the subtle night breeze painting goosebumps on our bare arms and legs as I told him what I've been trying to gather together since we got back. "For what it's worth, you helped me. You help me, present tense, too. And you with your determined attitude and your boldness will continue to in the future." I took a deep breath, looking up at the sky. You can almost see the stars tonight. "I just...I don't know, I suck at this, you know that, but thank you. Thank you for everything. Thank you for just being in my life." I told him, getting a little misty eyed as I looked back on how much progress we made in such a short time. "I think, meeting you was the best thing I have ever done."

He smiled his big, dimpley smile and pulled me into a bone-crushing hug, but I didn't care. We just stood there, under the almost-stars, our arms wrapped around each other, saying nothing, but feeling invincible as young gods.

Alex

I got home that night at around 11, and of course my parents paid no attention. They really did believe I was staying with a friend this whole time. Jordyn, of course, didn't, and interrogated me as soon as I walked through the door.

"Where have you been?"

"At a friends."

"For three nights?" She scrunched her face up at me, refusing to blink.

"....Yes."

"You really expect me to believe that?" She asked, leading me up to my room when she noticed my parents were coming in the room.

I flopped down on my bed and shivered, boarding my window back up with a thick piece of stray plywood I found a couple months ago.

"It's a long story."

"I got time." She sat down on my bed, patting the spot next to her. I rolled my eyes, knowing that she means well but she'll never give this up, so I told her. Everything. About Kat, ending the Felicia fiasco, stealing a plant, the weird cop with a mysterious past who saved our ass, the night we left, times square, the first hotel, the private beach, the ferris wheel, the second hotel, Monica and Stew Leonards. Our very own personal pie of a grand adventure.

She, Like Mrs. Rudntisky, was pissed I didn't tell her, but was ultimately proud of me. She just smiled, and gave me a big hug. I think I've given more hugs today than I ever have.

"I don't know if I ever properly told you this, but," She wiped happy tears from her eyes, mine starting to prick with them too. "I'm really glad that out of all the people who could have been my older brother, I got stuck with you."

"I'm really happy I got stuck with you, too." I told her, feeling almost exhausted from all the emotion of today.

"You better get some rest, dude," She says, getting up. "Graduation's in two days."

Shit. That's right.

A less-than-quarter-life-crisis may be due. Great.

No, I'm not gonna do this to myself. I'm not gonna think about that. I just came back from a spontaneous ass trip that was probably the most fun I've ever had in my life; I'm not gonna give the rapid, cruel movement of time the satisfaction of ruining that for me.

I didn't even bother to say hi to my parents as I put the tv on, falling asleep to the sound of terrible 90s sitcoms.

I woke up the next day to the bright June sun in my eyes and did absolutely nothing. Told my parents I was at my friend Anthony's this whole time. Surprise, surprise, they didn't question it. I went outside for a bit, watered the plants and talked to the old man next door. I called Matt to see if he wanted to catch up, but apparently he went with a bunch of other seniors to this "mixer" on coney island.

So I went back inside and watched movies, trying not to think too much about tomorrow. Yeah, my high school days are over, but isn't that a *good* thing? It means I'm being faced with the monster of adulthood with no survival kit, but it also means the thing i've wanted for so long; freedom. Maybe, just maybe, this will be good for me.

And I'm still young. I think it's time for me to start enjoying where I'm at; not looking to the past or future for comfort or anxiety, now, this very moment, where I'm alive.

I texted that to Kat and she told me that I was right, and that's something she needs to remember herself, too.

I smiled and continued my netflix day with *The Life Aquatic* and eventually fell asleep to the sound of the tv again, knowing that when I wake up, I'll be the same person I was yesterday- regardless of what is ending.

I woke up first, before the sun was even fully up. I quietly walked out the door and sat on the steps in front of my house, watching the sun rise over the trees and buildings. I just sat there, listening to nothing but the birds and the cars occasionally pass by, blaring morning new wave 80's channels.

This day was gonna be good.

I refuse to let it be something bad.

As I sat and thought about everything, Kat texted me.

Of course she's up.

She asked me if I was, and I just called her in response. She told me she couldn't go back to sleep, and that she wanted to come to the ceremony today. I smiled at that, knowing she wanted me to share this milestone with her, as we've shared many tiny ones in the past week.

I couldn't wait to see her again, honestly. It's only been two days but we accomplished something so big together that I feel like, in a cheesy ass way, that when we're together, we can do anything.

I stayed out there for what felt like an hour, until Jordyn came outside and said that I should get ready.

I panicked for a little bit, not remembering where I put my cap and gown. Jordyn must have heard me swearing because she walked into my room with both in hand. I thanked her and took a deep breath, putting them both on over one of my nice shirts and black jeans.

I looked at myself in the mirror, giggling hysterically.

I looked like a blue blob.

Why must we keep this cruel ass tradition?

I took the cap off for now and headed downstairs, where my parents were arguing while getting themselves ready.

I just rolled my eyes and told Jordyn I'd be back outside.

I waited out the next hour or so back on my porch, waving at my neighbors that were looking at me weird. Kat had told me that Ariel is coming to pick her up in ten minutes, so at least I have that to look forward to.

My parents came outside in a frenzy, rushing me and Jordyn to the car in fear of being late. We got to the school in a matter of five minutes, my family heading to the bleachers while I go into the planetarium, where the whole senior class is waiting to walk out from.

I found Matt in the sea of blue blobs by his newly dyed burgundy-red hair and sat next to him. He saw me and reached into the pocket of his pants under his gown, pulling out a little bottle of schnapps and wiggling his eyebrows. I kindly declined, as he just said "suit yourself," and downed the whole thing with a quiet WOO!

Our gym teacher lined us up in alphabetical order, meaning I got forced to the back of the line separated from morning tipsy Matt.

The sunlight was blinding, and the 11th grade marching band was obnoxiously loud with the graduation theme. We sat on the folded chairs on the football field as everyone's parents desperately tried to get pictures of their kids.

The dumb awards and superlatives came first, and of course I didn't get anything, but I was okay with that. I don't need to fit into this school's criteria of excellence, anyway. I'll make my own.

Felicia got her award for being "Most Sociable," and I just fuckin laughed at her. How pathetic is that. Imagine being remembered for something so trivial.

No, not gonna do that. I'm not bitter anymore. Promise.

After what felt like forever, they finally started giving out the diplomas. Matt put his middle fingers in the air once he got is, and in return he was cheered on and booed. They finally got to my name, and my breath caught in my throat as I walked toward the podium near the goalpost to my fresh future. My hands shook with both nerves and anticipation and I could feel my pulse hammering in the back of my head. The walk wasn't even that long, but I felt the path stretching out before me, the trees and the people closing in on me. I caught a glimpse of Kat, though, sitting by the edge of the bleachers, with her camera in hand. I smiled slightly and took my diploma, shaking my principal's hand.

A few moments later, we threw our caps into the cloud-less sky and didn't bother to pick them up after.

So, this is how it ends.

And this is how it starts.

My new life starts.

My new life starts, not with a bang, not with a whimper, but with an encouraging applause from my new best friend and the biggest smile my face could handle.

Just like it should be.

Kat

I ran up to Alex when the ceremony ended, him catching my camera after I tripped over my own foot.

"How do you feel?" I asked him, already knowing the answer.

"I…" He furrowed his eyebrows, licking his lips and pondering what he was about to say. "I feel free, I guess."

"Do you wanna drive back with us?" Ariel asked him, bouncing excitedly on the heels of her feet. "We're gonna find somewhere to eat, maybe take a little detour adventure."

Alex smiled and told us that he just needed to let Jordyn, his little sister, know where he's going.

After a few minutes, Alex, Matt, Ariel and I were all hopping over the gate that separated the field from the parking lot (cause it's more fun that way).

We ran over to Ariel's red convertible, Alex and I getting in the backseat with haste, not caring about the heat on the white leather. Matt pulled another bottle out of his robe as he got into the passenger's seat and Ariel started pulling away, shouting "WE'RE FREE, ASSHOLES!"

Ariel just laughed at him, putting on the radio, and I couldn't believe what I heard.

They were playing actual music.....not EDM.....on the radio.

Once Matt realized it was *I Melt With You* by Modern English, he leant down to turn it up over Alex screaming "THIS SONG MAKES ME FEEL THINGS!"

I don't know how, or why, but all of a sudden Alex unbuckled his seatbelt and put his hands in the air, sitting on the top of the seat on a main road, laughing his ass off.

I got my camera out to start filming, but then I had a better idea.

I set it in between Matt and Ariel's seat, and imitated the same pose alex was doing, leaning on the back of the car, taking in the sun on my face, and the buildings scraping into the sky, passing by in glimpses. I thought about the last month, who I am now, and where I'm at in terms of my mental health, my personality, my friendships.

And, God, Do I like where I am now.

Because, and I never thought I'd say this, Matt's right.

We are free.

We are alive.

We are now champions.

Not for once, but for now, and however long we want to be.

And as we abruptly opened our eyes and saw Ariel leaning over to kiss Matt, screaming "EYES ON THE ROAD" in unison, I had one thought. One thought that I haven't thought in a long time.

I love these people.

5 years later.

June 15th, 2023, 11:38 PM.

Kat is the only one left sitting in the small indie theater, actually watching the credits roll this time, admiring the fact that she had a say in each one. That she made this movie, as small as it was, when she was fresh out of college. She made a whole movie, with the small budget of 8 grand- about the best time of her life, and the best person she had ever met.

As soon as she was about to get up, make sure her parents and friends got home okay, she heard footsteps sink into the red carpeting.

She whipped her head around quickly, her freshly cut curls almost smacking her in the face.

There he was. His hair was still blonde and curly, but it was shorter now, giving him a weird aura of sophistication along with the suit he was wearing that she never thought she'd see in him. All of that went away, though, when he pulled his ukulele out from behind his back.

"Alex?" She questioned, even though she already knew it was him. She had a habit of clarifying everything, even the obvious. "You're here?"

At that, he giggled, a sound she hadn't heard in awhile. "Of course I am," He sat beside her, playing with the strings on his ukulele. "I'm sorry I'm late, my flight got delayed and it was this whole thing-"

"Don't worry about it." Kat told him, just happy that he was there. She had sent him an invitation to the premiere, but didn't expect him to come. He had moved to LA two years ago, after graduating from Eastman to pursue music. He was now playing guitar (and occasional ukulele) in what started as a new wave cover band, but he suggested they write their own music, and now they're known as a small indie rock band called The Brickheads.

"Do you mind starting it over for me?" He half-joked, but Kat had already made her way over to the projector, screening the movie again.

The words *THE LIVING LIST* flashed on the screen in bold yellow letters, as Alex gasped. "I remember those things!"

"Yeah, of course you do," Kat rested her head back against the leather seat, feeling tired as ever, but wanting with all her might to stay up all night. "We never finished them, but we did live like heroes, you know. Even just for a little bit, the effects of our time together festered in ways that inspired both of us."

"And look at us now," He says, looking at her with a proud smile. "The only way to go from here is up."

"That it is." Kat says, giving him a high five. "I can't wait to see what else The Life of Champions has in store for us."

Alex's eyes stung with happy tears as she mentioned the phrase she first said to him that night when they were both at their worst, deciding they deserved more.

"We were right," Alex mumbled, to no one but her. "We're invincible."

Kat beamed, a smile that Alex had not seen in the longest time, the one that lit up the lightning inside of her as she took his hand, glancing at the pinky ring he kept wearing; the same one he slipped into her pocket the night they met, not even paying attention to the movie. They'll watch it another time. "We'll always be.

Author's Note

(Or a Random Monologue From a Girl Who Still Can't Take Herself Seriously Enough for the Title of 'Author')

Well shit.

You made it this far.

If you're taking the time to read this, I just wanna say first and foremost, thank you. This book took two (and a half) years, two therapists, more than about ten breakdowns, nine sitcom binges, five albums that helped inspire this story, and literally everything in the fast-paced, cluttered, messy interstate highway that is my mind.

I started this book when I was 15. I got the idea from realizing the reality of my boring, newly homeschooled, depressed and anxious life- and I wanted, like all people, something more. I felt alone. Yeah, I have friends, but no one will understand me the way Kat and Alex do. I feel as though I'll never be able to be understood by anyone, so at least I have my own characters. Of course, everything in this book is YOUR interpretation, but to me, Kat is truly me, in all of her thoughts and feelings, in the way I'm getting better, the way I am a girl with a black cloud hanging over her head that the sun is slowly trying to sneak out of. Alex is the kind of friend I am. Alex finds happiness in the people that surround him, even if they unintentionally make him feel alone. Both of them are what I wish would happen to me, feeling like I'm truly alive instead of a zombie crawling out from my bedroom every once in awhile. I wrote these characters to make myself feel less alone, feel less like background noise, less like a chunk of senseless flesh and bone floating through time and space. Now, at the time of writing this, I'm 17, almost 18, feeling like time is going way too fast, desperately wanting to slow down and stay young, a little less depressed, a little less anxious, a little more alive as of this summer, and maybe a little less alone. But there are days, even whole weeks when I feel as though I have grey-colored glasses stuck on me, that I can't see anything good anymore, I can't see life in the amazing colors everyone else raves about.

I wrote this story for those times. For the times when you feel like you're drowning, suffocating, stuck in the same place. For the times when you feel empty, or when you're going to overflow. For when you feel like life is going too slow or too fast and you just want everything to slow down for a second. For when you feel like you're running out of time. For when you're scared of your future. For when you're bored. For when you're sad. For when you feel like you're gonna go nowhere in life. For when you feel, here's this word again, alone. Because even when that monster hiding under your brain convinces you that you are, you have to realize that you're not; and you never will be. As long as you have this book, which is a whole encapsulation of myself, you have someone by your side, rooting for you.

Which is another reason why I made this book. When I was diagnosed with the triple whammy-depression, OCD & anxiety, no one was talking about it. I felt like I was the only one with these paralyzing thoughts and feelings, the only one with a self sabotaging brain.
It's important for kids with mental illness to have something to fall back on, to have something to make them feel less alone, to have something there for them that would understand. Which I didn't. So,

I took matters into my own hands and created it myself. Even though I put effort into making this story fairly lighthearted and encouraging, mental illness is a serious and heavy issue that we need to spend more time discussing, not glorifying. I hope that this book opens the minds of at least one person, or could inspire or help them. This book is made to get people talking, this book is made for people to recognize that this is a normal thing that happens to a lot more teenagers than you know. This book is for lonely 14 year old me to get the representation she deserved. This book is for kids with mental illness to see themselves in a powerful light, for a change; to paint them as the conquerors and warriors that we are. We deserve happy journeys with happy endings too; and even though it might not feel like it at times, that's what we will get. We deserve the life of champions.

Of course, there's a lot of people I have to thank for helping me make this happen. There's my number one support system, my family- constantly proofreading, reviewing and telling me I shouldn't give up, that I can really make something out of this. My best friends, my number one source of inspiration, all of which I name-dropped in here one way or another, for always rooting for me and making me feel like gold when i'm convinced i'm just rusty metal. For truly teaching me how to be alive, running through streets and shining under streetlights I learned that the best thing I could ever do was be with you- so I wrote a book about it. My friend in South Carolina who became my friend a little before writing this, being my #1 source of support and has been by my side the whole way If there is anyone out there that could really be my platonic soulmate, she is it beyond a shadow of a doubt. Believe it or not, my therapist, for helping me follow through with this and making me realize I could live like my characters, too. My 7th grade english teacher who first got me interested into grandiose storytelling with his 2nd period screening of *The Truman Show* and jokes about hard drugs (don't ask). My groupchat, filled with amazing girls from all around the country that I met through a mutual appreciation of the same band. They always hype me up and give me feedback, sharing their insight, camaraderie and kindness with me as brain food. And finally, that very band, for releasing an album last February that encapsulated my thoughts and feelings, furthermore being a perfect soundtrack this story. This very album came to me at the right time, right when I was about to give up on this book, but it inspired me to keep going with it. I'll stay a zombie kid forever. Also, you- for still continuing to read way past the epilogue. Thank you for being interested in this story I cooked up in the very cloudy depths of my mind, I never thought anyone except me would get it. As a gift, I want to give you something I make best- a playlist. Here are some songs that I listened to while writing this story, that serve as a semi-official soundtrack to this small yet significant journey.

1. Souls - Hippo Campus
2. American Money - BØRNS
3. Ribs - Lorde
4. Vacation - Hippo Campus
5. Last Hope - Paramore
6. Sea Of Dreams - Oberhofer
7. Sunrise - Diners
8. Perfect Places - Lorde
9. I Wanna Get Better - Bleachers
10. Teenage Icon - The Vaccines
11. Youth - Glass Animals
12. Don't Cry, 2020 - COIN
13. Baseball - Hippo Campus
14. Thunder - Imagine Dragons
15. Memories - Weezer
16. Warm Glow - Hippo Campus
17. Slow March - K.Flay
18. Team - Lorde
19. Coming of Age - Foster the People
20. South - Hippo Campus

Now, go live. Go be invincible. Feel everything or nothing, whatever you choose. Think in glory and a little power. Set the hero rumbling through your chest and buzzing through your veins run free.

CPSIA information can be obtained
at www.ICGtesting.com
Printed in the USA
BVOW08s0448201217
503305BV00024B/3342/P